Meet Me in Malta

JOY SKYE

vinci
BOOKS

Vinci Books

vinci-books.com

Published by Vinci Books Ltd in 2026

1

This work is a work of fiction. Names, characters, places and incidents are the product of the author's imagination or are used fictitiously. Any resemblance to actual persons, living or dead, places and incidents is entirely coincidental.

A CIP catalogue record for this book is available from the British Library.

Paperback ISBN: 9781036710958

The EU GPSR authorised representative is Logos Europe, 9 rue Nicolas Poussion, 17000 La Rochelle, France contact@logoseurope.eu

By Joy Skye

Sublime Retreats Romances

Corfu Capers

Clueless in Croatia

Falling in Florence

Summer in San Sebastian

Lighting up Loveland

Meet Me in Malta

Moonlight Over Morocco

Chapter One

Belinda McGuire examined her face in the mirror above her vanity unit, searching for the inevitable signs of stress that the last few months had wrought on her in new, fine lines around her eyes. Discovering your husband of twenty-five years was a liar and a cheat was bad enough. Discovering that he'd already started a new family with a woman, well girl really, twenty years younger than yourself just before your 50th birthday was a blow too far.

She glanced around the room, ignoring the empty racks and shelves in the walk-in wardrobe where his clothes used to be, and debated redecorating. She'd never particularly liked Mike's taste in décor, but had gone along with it, as she had with most of his choices. But now the drab greys and pale blues he'd thought so chic depressed her even more.

Snapping out of her funk, she walked downstairs, examining their charming brownstone with fresh eyes, considering her options whilst ignoring the many spaces where pictures used to hang. She loved living on Beacon Hill, but now, with the kids and her husband gone, the house seemed excessive. It was definitely time for a change, but she felt too overwhelmed to make any positive decisions right now. Belinda made her way into the kitchen and turned on the ridiculously complicated coffee machine her husband had insisted on, to warm up.

She was flicking through her phone when it rang, but not before a familiar, colourful image snagged her attention.

'Morning, sweet cheeks,' cried Carla, her best friend and longtime rock. 'How are things in sunny Boston?'

'Not so sweet or sunny,' she replied sourly, putting her on speaker so she could examine the email that had caught her eye.

'Ah, hang in there, honey. Things are going to be so much better in a couple of months, you'll wonder what the fuss was about!'

'I doubt that very much,' Belinda retorted, but could not keep the smile from her face at Carla's continuous optimism.

'Listen, I know it's probably the last thing on your mind. But I wanted to check what you were doing about the party for your birthday next month?'

'Good grief, I'm cancelling that! Half the people won't come because they're Mike's friends; the other half will only come to gawk at me and offer those horribly sincere "poor you" faces while they talk about me behind my back.'

'I figured as much,' Carla laughed. 'So, what d'ya wanna do? Shall I book us a spa retreat somewhere or something? We have to do something to mark the occasion.'

'I'm not sure I have to.' She stated flatly. 'But I could certainly do with getting away for a while.'

The email from Sublime Retreats, highlighting their

latest villa in Valletta, had brought back vivid memories of her childhood. Summers spent in Malta, before her mom met and married an oil tycoon from Texas and he whisked them off to start a new life, were some of the happiest times in her life. The vivid photographs of azure seas, faded baroque facades on waterfront settings, and incredible yachts lining the docks tugged at something in her soul.

'Just tell me what you need,' Carla continued. 'A break in Cabo, a quick blast in the Bahamas. Whatever you fancy!'

'I'm going to book a villa in Malta. For a month,' Belinda said, surprising herself. 'That way, anyone who genuinely wants to help me celebrate can jolly well make an effort and get themselves out there!'

There was a brief pause. 'Well, I have to say I'm loving this new, decisive Belinda,' exclaimed Carla. 'You can definitely count me in for at least two weeks. Let me know the dates and I'll see what I can do.'

Ending the call and pressing the button to start the much-needed shot of coffee pouring, Belinda warmed to her spontaneous idea. Why the hell not? Mike would hardly be using the travel club with a baby on the way, and letting her use their days with the club up was the least he could do in the circumstances. And going back to Malta had always been a dream of hers. Her grandparents had passed away a few years ago, but she would love to visit their graves and place flowers. She'd hated not being able to get back for the funerals.

An image of Noah floated up; she hadn't thought about him in years. Her grandparent's neighbor's son had become her sidekick during those summers, despite being several years younger. His permanent chubby cheeky grin, sparkling green eyes and love of adventures made him the perfect companion as they ran wild around the local area. Idly wondering where he might be now, she emailed Sublime Retreats to book the villa almost reflexively. It was a renovated historic property, perched on the waterfront with stunning views and all the facilities you could wish for, including a heated pool and hot tub. With four bedrooms, she'd either be rattling around in it herself, or the kids and or friends could join her. It was better than rattling around the brownstone on her milestone birthday.

The details were confirmed with surprising alacrity. A week from today the villa was hers for four weeks. Ignoring the increasingly hysterical messages from Mike, who was automatically included in the correspondence, demanding to know what the hell she was doing, Belinda booked the flights, and a private driver for the month. Charging it all to their joint credit card.

Settling into a comfortable chair in the snug, always her favourite room in the house with a view of the harbor, she spent some time composing an email. Including her children as a given, she deliberated over who else to cc into the missive. It was quite eye-opening to realise how few people from her current friend group she would actually want to be cooped up with, even in a fantastic villa in a stunning location. A last moment of whimsy made her add her sister's email address. Being ten years older, Susan had already left the nest when their mom decided to emigrate with the new love of her life. In the last thirty-eight years, they'd seen each other exactly twice. The first time, Belinda had travelled to England with their mom for Susan's wedding. The second, Susan had, seemingly reluctantly, joined her for Mom's funeral. Yes, they exchanged messages for birthdays and whatnot, but not exactly what you'd call a close sibling relationship.

Closing the laptop with a satisfied snap, Belinda let out a long breath, a small bubble of excitement welling up. After weeks of turmoil, self-doubt and indecision, she finally had a plan.

What had she done?

Chapter Two

Carla's response was, unsurprisingly, enthusiastic and immediate.

Count me in for the first two weeks—longer if I can wangle it. Let me know the flight details; I'll fly with you. If you haven't already, let's book first class. We're celebrating, remember? Freedom and turning fifty!

They'd met at school when she first arrived in America, and Carla had been the only thing that made sense in this new, big, alien world. Being dragged away from the only life, school and friends she had known at the age of twelve had been terrifying. In an environment that was completely at odds with her English upbringing, and so far away from her Maltese connections she felt dizzy, Carla had been an oasis of normality. Slightly crazy normality to be sure. But it worked, and their friendship was set in stone pretty much from day one. Smiling at the screen, Belinda sent through her flights, already first class, on Mike's dime, obviously.

If Carla was coming, that was enough. She'd be happy by herself for a time, rediscovering favourite places in

Malta, soaking up the wonderful atmosphere of Valletta and enjoying reliving her youth, not to mention the amazing food. Belinda realised she was more excited about the prospect of this trip than she had been about the two hundred people, black-tie event that had been planned to celebrate her birthday. As much as she loved organizing events like this, calling on her eye for detail and meticulous planning skills, it had never felt like *her* event. In fact, she felt relieved that she wouldn't have to go through with the whole charade.

Next, was a prompt, if vague, message from her eldest, Jason. He was a high flyer in New York, doing something terribly clever in finance; she'd never really understood what. He and his impossibly beautiful wife, Alicia, always seemed to be extremely busy. So, she didn't hold out much hope of them joining her, despite his assurances of checking calendars, but she appreciated the effort.

She knew her daughter Annalise would be slower to respond. Completely opposite in character to her brother, she was a free-spirited artist who kept very strange hours. Her muse striking at odd times of the day, she sometimes holed up in her studio for worrying periods of time when there was no communication at all. Belinda had had to learn not to panic on these occasions and never admitted to the number of times she'd nearly booked flights to San Francisco to beat down the door and check she was okay. But Annalise always surfaced eventually, with a beatific smile on her face and full of excitement for her latest work.

Another email pinged, this time from the concierge at the villa. She marveled at the efficiency of the company and its employees. It was the main reason they had joined the club, that and the kudos Mike felt it lent them.

From: sophia.a@sublimeretreats.com
To: BelleMc@gmail.com
Dear Mrs McGuire,
I am delighted to see you will be joining us for four wonderful weeks at Villa Veduti tal-baħar in Valletta.
My name is Sophia, and I will be your dedicated host throughout your stay. I am available 24/7 to make sure your vacation runs as smoothly as possible.
I have attached a list of great activities and wonderful restaurants so we can start planning your time.
Please send me your flight details and guest list so we can prepare the villa for your arrival, and do let me know if you need assistance with transfers.
Villa Veduti tal-baħar comes with a dedicated chef who caters for breakfasts and either lunch or dinner for you. I have also attached his menu, although as you are here for an extended period, he will happily discuss other options with you. Please note that he had one day off a week.
And finally, please send a grocery list if you would like me to pre-stock the villa for you and your guests.
Best regards,
Sophia

To: sophia.a@sublimeretreats.com
From: BelleMc@gmail.com
Dear Sophia,
Thank you so much for your email. I am very excited to visit beautiful Malta once again.
My friend Carla and I arrive at 10:00pm on flight LH421. I have booked a driver for the month, so no assistance is needed for transfers. As for the other guests, I am still waiting for confirmation. I imagine I will have various members of my family, etc. coming and going, but we shall

see. I will keep you updated; hopefully, we won't be too difficult for you!
As we have the chef covering breakfast plus another meal, I am looking forward to visiting the food market to buy fresh produce and cooking a little myself. I have attached a list of some wines and champagne we would like to start us off. And please add a few cases of bottled water, both still and sparkling. As we are arriving so late, if the chef can just leave a cold platter or similar for us, that would be great.
If I think of anything else, I will let you know. Otherwise, I look forward to meeting you next week.
Belinda

The next week flew by as she made preparations to leave for a month, cancelling appointments, arranging for the cleaner to come in daily to water her plants and, of course, shopping. Carla had insisted she buy herself a new wardrobe for the trip. It was quite liberating being able to shop freely, not having to consider Mike's conservative tastes, and she found herself drawn to the bright colours and patterns that he would hate. To finish off, she treated herself to a new set of matching luggage in bright fuchsia. You certainly couldn't miss that on the luggage belt, she giggled to herself, almost giddy with growing excitement.

Chapter Three

Sophia let herself in through the side door of the villa on the morning of her next arrival, to see off the departing guests and start the preparation for the incoming. Although with just two people arriving, it should be a fairly quiet few weeks. They'd had a group of eight old college friends from Texas this last week, here celebrating various anniversaries. They were a fun, high-spirited group that had certainly kept the chef and housekeeper busy, but at least Mrs McGuire wasn't landing until tonight, so they had all day to return the villa to the pristine condition expected by club members.

'Morning, Chef!' she called loudly as she walked into the kitchen so as not to startle him. He liked to listen to music while he worked, so always had earbuds in when guests weren't in front of him. He paused mid-washing up, dried his hands carefully and removed one bud.

'Good morning, Sophia. The guests are just collecting their luggage, they should be down and ready to go on time,' he replied cheerfully with the grin that set most of the ladies' hearts fluttering. Noah was over six feet tall, movie star handsome and, despite being somewhere in his forties, in extremely good shape. Sophia was twenty-five, so he was far too old for her, but she could certainly appreciate the aesthetic. It also provided her with endless entertainment as each week, at least one of the women or sometimes men in the villa fell madly in love with him.

All Sophia cared about was the fact that he was an amazing chef, and happily conceded to all the weird and wonderful food fads and allergies that cropped up each week. Only grumbling quietly to her once they were out of earshot. He could be a bit brusque, some might say moody, but he was the best chef she'd worked with and the guests loved him. Sophia knew he had repeated, lucrative offers from the top restaurant on Gozo Island, but luckily, he opted to stay with them.

'So, we just have two arriving today?' he asked with a raised eyebrow. 'For a month? That's a bit unusual.'

'It is strange, and all very last minute. But she sounded lovely in her email. So, yes, only two arrive today. There may be more coming later, I'll give you as much notice as I can,' she told him. 'Here are their contact details.' She handed him the sheet of paper she pulled from her bag.

'Hmph,' his face soured. 'Whenever you say they sound lovely, they turn out to be the most work.'

She laughed. 'It's just two ladies; how much trouble can they be?'

Noah didn't look convinced but continued, 'I'll finish cleaning up this lot,' he waved a hand to take in the mounds of dishes waiting to be cleaned. 'Then I'll go to get the supplies for the next few days.'

'Great, I'll meet them tonight, so just leave the platter

ready in the fridge and you can find out how much trouble they are in the morning!'

'Hilarious,' he scowled, then grinned again and returned the bud to his ear and continued with the task at hand.

Noah loved these moments; left to his own devices to do the work he loved with his favourite tunes blasting away. It kept his mind wandering to darker times, things he didn't want to remember. Keeping busy, blocking out the world with music as he worked, was the best remedy he'd found.

Once the kitchen was spick and span, he did a quick inventory and made a list of what he needed from the market. Outside in the morning air, he took a moment to appreciate the clear bright skies and the incredible blues of the water between the villa and Manoel Island. Several small fishing boats bobbed merrily in the slight swell caused by the regular breeze that meant the terrace was always comfortable. Taking in a deep breath, he clipped on his helmet and jumped on his moped, zooming off down familiar, narrow back streets to his local market.

Being a Saturday, it was already busy, but Noah knew the place like the back of his hand and easily weaved his way through the throng to his favourite stalls. The air buzzed with chatter and laughter, mingling with the hum of haggling voices and the rhythmic clatter of crates being unpacked. Bright awnings stretched overhead, casting patches of red, yellow, and blue across the cobblestones. The scent of freshly baked bread drifted from a nearby bakery stall, mixing with the sharp tang of citrus and the earthy aroma of spices. Pyramids of oranges glowed like tiny suns beside heaps of glossy aubergines and bunches of wildflowers tied with twine. Street musicians played an upbeat tune, its notes weaving through the crowd as vendors called out cheerful greetings to familiar faces. To Noah, this market wasn't just a place to shop; it was a living, breathing tapestry of colour, sound, and life.

'Good morning, Mikiel,' he called when he reached the fish stall. 'Catch anything good today?'

Mikiel's tanned, wrinkled face lit up when he saw him. 'I always catch something good, my boy. Your cheekiness has been your issue since you were this big,' he replied, holding a hand down at thigh level. Mikiel had been his father's best friend, and acted like an uncle to him, as well as providing the best fish in the area. After much good-natured wrangling, Noah came away with the lampuki and tuna that he needed to try out a new recipe, before working his way around his regular route, chatting with stallholders and picking up the fresh produce, cheeses and meats that were on his list.

After a quick coffee, he whizzed back to the villa, shopping safely in the panniers of his bike, feeling almost cheerful. An entire month with just a couple of guests meant light work for him. He'd have more time for his volunteer work. Maybe he'd have time to work on his house, which had been an ongoing project for so many years that it had become a good-natured joke between his friends. Maybe he would finally clear out that room, the one he never went in because it held too many memories. Shaking his head to deflect that train of thought, he unloaded the shopping and started to unpack and put it away. *Let's see how these two are in the morning,* he thought to himself. *After all, as Sophia said, how much trouble could two women be?*

Chapter Four

When Carla spotted Belinda at Logan Airport, she let out a whoop that could be heard along the concourse and caused people to turn and stare. She dropped everything and bounded up, embracing her in a hug that made her ribs hurt.

'Calm down, loony,' she said affectionately, returning the squeeze for several long minutes.

'I will not calm down! Me and my bestie are off on an adventure, and we're both young, free and single.' She arched back to look up at her and waggled her eyebrows suggestively.

Carla had lost her husband to cancer five years ago, but after the initial grief and mourning had passed, she pulled herself together and seemed even more determined to wring every drop of joy out of life that she could. Despite the late hour, Carla managed to look as stylish as ever. Her tiny, svelte five-foot frame was encased in soft grey leggings and a combination of layered tops in shades of blue that brought out her eyes.

'I'm not sure how adventurous I'm feeling right now, but what do you say to getting this lot checked in and grabbing a glass of something with bubbles in the lounge?'

'Hell yeah,' Carla cried, immediately letting her go and retrieving her luggage. Belinda took hold of the trolley with its towering pink pile of suitcases and wrestled it to the check-in desk. It didn't take long before they were in the lounge, settled on the comfortable leather sofas, raising a toast to the weeks ahead.

'So, tell me, Belinda,' said Carla after the initial flurry of catching up. 'How are you doing? I mean, really?'

She paused mid-sip and gave it some thought. This wasn't a casual enquiry from nosy acquaintances that she could respond with a flippant, "Oh, I'm fine." 'Actually, I'm doing okay, surprisingly,' Belinda replied, realising it was true. 'I mean, my whole life is upside down, and I have no idea what I'll do next, which is scary. But I don't really miss Mike, you know? Not like you'd think.'

'Well, he wasn't really around much these last years, was he, honey?'

'True, and now we know why.' she laughed mirthlessly. 'But even that doesn't hurt so much anymore. I still think he's a bastard, but he's not my problem anymore, so that's a bonus.'

'Atta girl. You keep that up. These things take time. You were married for a long time; it will take you a while to find your feet and discover yourself again.' Carla looked at her steadily, her eyes expressing what she didn't need to say out loud. Belinda leant over and squeezed her hand; she knew her friend was speaking from experience.

At that moment, an attendant appeared like magic by their table with a bottle held aloft to top up the glasses. 'I just need to inform you, Mrs McGuire, that there is a delay to your flight. A minor technical issue, but hopefully it won't take too long.'

Belinda became aware of the grumbling of the other passengers in the lounge, one man in a business suit up at the desk gesticulating wildly, obviously unimpressed with this development. 'Don't you worry,' Belinda smiled at the nervous-looking woman. 'We've got a four-hour layover after this flight, so just keep these topped up and you won't hear any complaints from us.'

The two friends continued to chat happily. It had been months since they were last together, and barely noticed the time fly by, let alone the fact the plane was nearly three hours late taking off. Fueled by more glasses of champagne than they would usually partake of before a flight, they both slept soundly for the entire seven hours it took to get to Frankfurt.

A steward woke them discreetly as they were coming in to land. 'Good morning, I just wanted to inform you, as you have a connecting flight quite soon, a member of staff will be on hand as you disembark to take you straight to your next gate.'

Blearily, Belinda looked up at him. It took a moment for her brain to catch up with her surroundings, then she prodded Carla, who was drifting off again. 'Come on, sleepyhead, wakey, wakey. We've got another plane to catch in…' she looked enquiringly at the attendant.

'About an hour,' he admitted sheepishly. 'But don't worry, we'll get you there.'

They were given priority and rushed off the plane, where a sturdy woman in a grey uniform was waiting with a clipboard and a grim expression. 'On there,' she snapped, gesturing at the waiting buggy. Meekly obeying, the two friends had barely got themselves in the seat when the buggy took off like it was the start of the Grand Prix and flew down the never-ending corridors of Frankfurt Airport. Passengers on foot scattered as they sped along, the woman keeping her hand almost continuously on the horn, which made an annoying mournful beep. When they came to a skidding halt at their desk, Carla was grinning. 'I must get me one of these for the ranch! I might need bigger wheels though.'

They were the last ones to board; the captain was already making his announcements as they found their seats and buckled in and soon started taxiing down the runway. The last leg of the journey was a short two-hour flight, and fueled by copious amounts of coffee, they walked off the plane full of excitement for what lay ahead. Unfortunately, what lay ahead was the discovery that Belinda's luggage hadn't made it to Malta, and apparently was languishing somewhere back at Frankfurt.

'Oh, for God's sake,' Belinda moaned as she filled out the necessary form. 'All my lovely new clothes. How could they miss bright pink suitcases!'

'Don't you worry,' Carla reassured her. 'These things happen all the time, I'm sure they will be with you soon enough. For tonight, you can just borrow something of mine to sleep in.'

Belinda looked down at her friend's diminutive form, then pointedly down at her decidedly buxom five-foot nine frame. 'Not sure that's gonna work, Car.'

'Oh hush, it'll be fine,' she pushed her playfully. 'It's not my fault you're a giant.'

Resigning herself to the inevitable, Belinda shrugged. 'I guess it doesn't matter; no one else is going to see me, anyway.'

Chapter Five

When Belinda woke up the next morning, she realised from the throbbing of her head that drinking more champagne when they arrived, rather than eating the wonderful platter that had been laid out for them, was probably not a good idea. 'Oh, my stars,' she muttered as she rolled out of bed and staggered to the bathroom. One look in the mirror confirmed this had been, in fact, a terrible idea. Her hair looked like she'd been dragged through a hedge backwards, her brown curls a tangled mess. Yesterday's mascara had seeped below her bloodshot eyes, reminiscent of Alice Cooper, and the tiny t-shirt and shorts set Carla had lent her was doing nothing to cover her wobbly bits.

Right, she thought. Coffee. She traipsed out of her room, only now taking in the details of her surroundings. It was dark when they arrived, and despite Sophia, the concierge, showing them around the villa, she hadn't really paid much attention. The villa was absolutely stunning, and the bright Mediterranean sunshine was streaming through the arched windows, almost blinding her. Polished limestone walls glowed a soft honey-gold, their warm tones reflecting the light that poured in from every direction. Beyond the airy sitting room, elegant French doors opened onto a sweeping terrace, where an infinity pool shimmered like liquid glass against the backdrop of the deep blue sea. White linen curtains drifted lazily in the coastal breeze, carrying with them the faint scent of salt and blooming bougainvillea. Inside, every detail spoke of effortless luxury, cool marble floors, handcrafted Maltese tiles, and subtle touches of brass and olive wood that echoed the island's rich heritage. From the shaded pergola, she could glimpse the terracotta rooftops of a distant village, the church dome rising proudly above the horizon. It felt less like a house and more like a dream in her fuzzy state, carved from sunlight and stone. She made her way to where she vaguely remembered the kitchen was located but paused at the door. Unless her mind was playing tricks on her, the aromatic smell of freshly brewed coffee was in the air.

Cautiously pushing the door open, she peered into the kitchen. There was a man there, a rather large one at that. He had his back to her and was doing something on the countertop, oblivious to her presence. She was just deciding whether to scream or run when he started to move, a hand shot up in the air several times and then his butt, clad in tight-fitting jeans, began to wiggle, reminding her of Hugh Grant's famous scene in Love Actually. She stifled a giggle, her flight or fight instincts now totally appeased, as his body movements became more vigorous, ending in a twirl that brought them face to face.

'Il-Madonna!' he shouted, a hand flying to his chest, the spoon he was holding smearing something creamy across his chest, which she now realised was encased in an apron. Of course, it was the chef. She'd completely forgotten about that with one thing and another.

'I'm sorry,' she said, 'I didn't mean to startle you.' She walked towards him, smiling apologetically, proffering her hand. He didn't move to take it, just carefully put down the spoon and removed a set of earbuds and placed them next to it, all the while staring at her strangely. Feeling extremely uncomfortable, Belinda remembered with a sharp intake of breath what a state she looked like right now, and how much of her was on show. 'Sorry about this,' she waved her hands around. 'I know I look a fright; I'll just go and… well, go and sort myself out.'

She turned her blushing face quickly away and started for the door when he finally spoke.

'Belle?'

The deep voice she didn't recognise, but the nickname she did. There was only ever one person who called her that. Confused, she faced him again, taking in the tall frame, the handsome features and the shock of dark hair cropped close to his scalp. It was only when she focused on his eyes, those deep green eyes, that even now had a twinkle in them, that the penny dropped. 'Noah? Is that really you?'

'What are you doing here?' he demanded, sounding resentful, his handsome face screwed up in confusion.

'Looking for coffee,' she replied stupidly, her brain unable to take in the fact that cheeky little Noah had grown into… well, this gorgeous-looking man, despite the scowl on his face that was currently directed at her.

'I meant here, in this villa.'

Slightly affronted at this odd interrogation, she stood up straight and met his glare head-on. 'I'm here on holiday; I booked the villa. And I would like my coffee now if you don't mind,' she pointed to where the machine sat percolating on the counter. *What on earth was wrong with him?*

His eyes slid down briefly, reminding her that there was not much material covering her chest or anywhere else right now. Flushing again, she walked over and started to help herself to the much-needed caffeine.

'I should do that for you,' he said, but made no move to take over.

'What a coincidence, huh? I take it you're a chef now?' she called over her shoulder, trying to lighten the atmosphere.

'Well spotted. I take it you are Mrs McGuire,' he growled, not being drawn into her attempt at chit-chat.

With a sigh, Belinda took a swig of her coffee before responding. She couldn't deal with this bizarre situation right now. Her head was pounding; she had no idea what time it was and, quite frankly, his attitude was getting on her nerves. 'Yes, I am, Noah. I believe you will provide breakfast for myself and my guest?' Belinda could hear how snooty she sounded, but to hell with it. He was being a jerk, and she really needed a long hot shower, followed closely by something to eat.

He looked at her for a beat. 'Yup, it'll be served in an hour on the terrace.'

With that, he turned back to the counter, popped his earbuds back in and continued to stir whatever was in the bowl there. 'Conversation over, I guess,' she muttered to herself and quickly left the kitchen and the grumpy chef and headed back up to her room.

Her bathroom was amazing, artfully built around the dramatic arches of the historic stone structure, and thankfully the shower was hot and powerful. As she washed away the travel weariness and the vestiges of her hangover, she marveled at the pure quirk of fate that had put her here, in a villa that Noah worked in. I mean, what were the chances? And more to the point, what on earth had happened to him that had turned that eternally smiling boy she remembered into a grouchy man, albeit an annoyingly handsome one? She reflected on that for a moment. Despite the terse conversation, she would have to be blind not to notice how well his jeans and t-shirt fitted, the hint of a tattoo peeking out from the sleeve on his muscled biceps.

If she had thought about seeing him again, she would have imagined a joyful reunion full of laughter and reminiscing, not this oddly confrontational meeting. Toweling herself dry, Belinda decided not to dwell on it. It might make for some awkwardness, but there was no way she was going to let another man spoil her birthday treat. Remembering she had nothing to dress in, she pulled on one of the luxurious white robes, which was roomy enough to cover everything that had been on show earlier. Embarrassment flooded her again. God, what must he have thought? There she was, thinking about what had happened to him; he was probably thinking the same thing about her!

Chapter Six

Noah was in shock. As he went through the motions of preparing the fruit platters, getting the eggs ready to cook on demand and laying the table outside, he struggled to make sense of his feelings. He'd had such a crush on Belle when he was a boy. As summer approached, he would drive his parents insane, constantly asking when she and her mother would arrive for the holidays. He would follow her around like a puppy for the six weeks they were there, desperately trying to come up with more and more crazy things for them to do, just to see that smile and hear her laugh. His memories of those summers were filled with fun, endless warm days when they ran free, swimming at hidden beaches, camping out with food parcels from his parents, and one time stealing Mikiel's fishing boat to go exploring Manoel Island. That hadn't gone down so well, but it had been fun while it lasted.

Then, one year, she didn't come. His father explained that Belle's mother had met and married a man in America and they lived there now. His seven-year-old self didn't really understand how this could be possible, and despite his dad's assurances that they would surely visit again, they never did. Noah had been angry and miserable all that first summer without her, barely leaving his room. But time passed, life marched on the way it does, and eventually she became just a memory. Until this morning. When every angst ridden angry emotion he had felt back then bubbled up like a bottle of Coke with a Mento dropped in it and he hadn't been able to stop it.

It didn't help that she looked gorgeous. Belle had grown into a stunning-looking woman, her wild brown curls still playing havoc and that ridiculous tiny t-shirt she'd been wearing doing nothing to hide her womanly charms. Shaking his head to clear the image, Noah felt guilty. He hadn't thought about a woman in that way since Sarah. It had been five long years, but he had committed to loving her for the rest of his life. Belle didn't fit into that scenario; no one did.

Checking the table one last time to make sure he had everything ready, he saw another woman coming outside, her yawn turning into a wide smile when she saw him.

'Well, hello handsome,' she sing songed in a light Texan drawl. 'Have I died and gone to heaven?'

He gave her his brilliant multi-watt smile, which he knew won over even the sternest of guests. 'I'm pretty sure you're still alive and in Malta, which is very close.'

'That priest sure does suggest otherwise,' she murmured, her eyes flicking to the pool area where a young man in robes was poking about in the water.

He followed her gaze and laughed. 'That's just Ġakobb. He is in fact the pool boy, but currently in training to join the priesthood. He fits in his work around this, it may look a little…' he stopped, unsure of how to finish this sentence.

'Incongruous is the word you are reaching for, Honey. I thought he was here for my last rites, but no worries. This spread looks amazing. Have you seen any signs of Belinda yet? We had quite a late night.' She giggled as she said this and sat at the table, grabbing a pastry and reaching for the coffeepot.

'Briefly,' he said, walking back into the villa, trying not to think about it. When he returned with the basket of freshly cut bread, she was there. Of course, she was; where else would she be, he chided himself. Belle was chatting away with her friend, apparently unconcerned by his presence.

'Carla, have you met our chef, Noah?'

'I did see this handsome hunk before, but we weren't formally introduced,' the tiny blonde purred. 'I must say, the views here just get better and better.' Noah felt the heat rising to his cheeks. It wasn't unusual for guests to make appreciative comments about him, normally he would take it in his stride, even play up to it a little. But with Belle there, he felt awkward and uncomfortable. Belle gave her friend a sharp look.

'Leave him alone, Carla. He's here to cook for us, not provide you with entertainment!'

Carla just laughed and gave him a lascivious wink over her coffee cup.

'Eggs,' he said a little too loudly. 'Would either of you like some eggs?' he added in a more reasonable tone, trying to keep his face impassive.

'Sure would,' said Carla. 'Anyway you like, I'm easy,' she giggled.

Belle nodded. 'Yes, whatever's easy,' she said without looking at him. He hurried back to the safety of his kitchen, wondering how long he could stretch out hiding in there and fervently wishing he hadn't given his assistant the week off. Usually, he had someone else to do the service, but with just two guests, it hadn't seemed necessary. Much to his relief, Sophia bustled in through the back door at that moment.

'Morning chef. How are our guests this morning?'

'Hmph. Alive and eating breakfast out there,' he jutted his chin towards the terrace.

'As cheerful as ever, Noah,' she laughed. She was used to his grumpy ways and ignored it. 'I'll just go and have a chat with them.'

When he brought out the perfectly scrambled eggs, he caught the tail end of their conversation. 'So, my bags will arrive today?' Belle was asking, with a hopeful smile on her face.

'Yes,' Sophia confirmed. 'I spoke with the airline, and they are coming on a flight this morning. I'll get them picked up and delivered here for you.'

'Thank goodness for that. Trying to cram myself into Carla's gear was not a good look!'

That would explain the tiny outfit this morning, he thought, wordlessly placing the dish on the table and walking away as they began to discuss possible activities for the next few days. Hopefully, they would be out and about every day, although as they were here for a month it was inevitable they would spend some time relaxing at the villa. He raised his eyes to the heavens as confused emotions ran high. What have I done to deserve this? He pleaded silently. And how am I going to cope with seeing Belle every day?

Chapter Seven

Belinda watched Noah's retreating back, only half listening to the conversation between Carla and Sophia. She was still completely shaken by the fact that he was here. Tall, handsome and here in the villa she had booked for a month. It was insane. Her phone chimed with an incoming message. Picking it up, she saw it was yet another message from Mike.

'What's up, honey?' asked Carla, seeing the consternation on her face.

'Oh, it's another message from Mike. He keeps saying he wants to talk to me.'

'What on earth could that man think he has to say after everything he's done?' she scoffed.

Aware that Sophia was watching them curiously, Belinda changed the conversation. 'What do you want to do today, Carla? I can't go anywhere until my luggage arrives, so do you fancy chilling out here and then going into town for dinner?' Carla gave a luxuriant stretch like a cat in the sun.

'Sounds good to me. I've hung around worse places in my time,' she grinned.

'In that case, we should speak to Noah about what you would like for lunch,' Sophia told them. 'Have you discussed any menu options yet?'

Belinda's heart thudded at the thought of talking to Noah. He had reacted so weirdly to seeing her, and she really couldn't understand why. 'I'll go and have a chat with him now,' she said, deciding it was best to take the bull by the horns.

'I'm happy to chat with him if you like?' Carla said with an impish grin.

Belinda gave her a stern look as she pushed back her chair. 'You just sit there, missy,' she laughed. Carla really was incorrigible. Steeling herself, she made her way into the kitchen where she saw Noah was washing up some pans and the large butler sink. 'Noah,' she called, not wanting to startle him again. He glanced up, and a brief smile flickered across his face before dropping away.

'Hi, Belle. What can I do for you?' he asked in a reasonable tone. *Maybe he was thawing a bit?*

'Carla and I are planning to relax here today. At least until my clothes arrive, I can't very well go out naked, can I?' *Why the hell had she said that?* Yet again, she could feel the heat rising to her face. She seemed to spend her entire time looking like a beetroot around this man, whose eyes were now widened in surprise. 'So, we wondered if you could make us some lunch,' she hurried on. 'If that's okay,' she added lamely.

He sighed. 'Of course it's okay; it's my job after all,' he said in a tone that suggested he'd rather do anything else than prepare lunch for them. He opened a drawer and pulled out a folder, sliding it across the counter with a flick of his hand.

'Here's my menu. Let me know what you want,' he said as she just managed to catch it before it fell to the floor. *What I want is for you to stop being a dick*, she thought as she started to flip through the pages. It was an extensive menu filled with mouthwatering familiar names of dishes she hadn't thought about in years. She'd forgotten so much about her time here, she realised, but thirty-eight years would do that to a memory. Noah was staring at her expectantly, making it difficult to concentrate. She snapped the menu shut. 'Something light today as we'll be out for dinner. Maybe fish and a salad? You choose.'

'Sure. I'll go to the market and see what's good, although I seem to remember you love swordfish.'

Surprised, Belinda nodded. 'God yes, I haven't had a decent swordfish steak in years; that would be amazing.' She paused, lost in thought. 'Is Mikiel still fishing?'

A genuine smile lit up Noah's face. 'Yes, that old scoundrel will fish until he drops; he refuses to retire.' Responding to his show of affection, she smiled back at him.

'Tell him I said hello when you see him. And I'll catch up with him soon, just not today.'

'When you have some clothes to put on would definitely be better,' he grinned, looking more like the boy that she remembered. She giggled in acknowledgement. 'Are he and your father still joined at the hip?'

Noah's face fell, shutters coming down in an instant. 'My father passed away five years ago.'

'Oh, Noah. I'm sorry,' she told him. Bastjan had been a lovely man and a wonderful father, always ready with a smile and a joke no matter what trouble they had gotten into. He shrugged and put the menu folder back in the drawer, banging it shut.

'These things happen,' he said simply and turned to continue vigorously scrubbing a pan.

As she returned to the terrace, her mind was full of memories of people and places that had made up those glorious summer holidays. Maybe the loss of his father had affected Noah so much that his reaction to her was grief. His dad had brought him up single-handedly after his mother had run off with someone else. They had a tight-knit relationship, as much buddies as father and son, so it would have been a tremendous loss for him.

But that glimpse, that tiny flash of young Noah, told her he was still in there somewhere, and Belinda decided she would have to try to bring him out to play again.

Chapter Eight

As Noah headed to the market to visit Mikiel and the other stallholders to get the ingredients for lunch, his mind was full of memories of golden summer days, a long-limbed girl with wild curls and his unrequited crush on her. His old friend was there as always with a broad smile and a mountain of freshly caught fish displayed on his stall, which was one of the largest at the market.

'Morning, boy.' He called his familiar greeting as he came around to give him one of his bone-crushing hugs.

'Morning, old man,' he grinned back when he was finally released. 'I'm in need of some fine swordfish; any chance you can help?'

'Hmph. Of course, what a stupid question! How much do you need?'

'Just a couple of good-size steaks, I only have two guests at the moment.'

Mikiel busied himself selecting the fish, placing it on the waxed paper on the scales and ringing up the total on his ancient till. 'Only two? That's a bit odd, isn't it? They're going to be rattling around in that place.' Noah chuckled. Mikiel lived in a tiny cottage near the harbour where he kept his boat and couldn't for the life of him understand why anyone would need to spend good money on what he considered an oversized mansion. As far as he was concerned, all you needed for a happy life was the sun, the sea and the odd glass or two of Lumincetta.

'It is unusual,' Noah responded. 'And you'll never guess who the main guest is.'

'I guess by the smile on your face it's someone famous, that even I might have heard of?'

'Not even close,' he said, accepting the package of neatly wrapped fish steaks. 'It's Belle. Do you remember her?'

It took a moment, then the old man's face split into a wide grin and he gave a guffaw of laughter and slapped his thighs in merriment. 'Remember her? How could I forget? You rascals were the bane of my life back then. I still haven't forgiven you for stealing my boat,' he teased good-naturedly. 'I seem to recall you being madly in love with the girl; does she still make your heart sing?' he asked with a wink.

Noah, who was just putting the parcel in his bag, stopped and looked up with a scowl. 'What do you mean?' he asked defensively.

'Now, now, boy. Don't get all agitated. It was as plain as the nose on your face that you were totally smitten with the girl. Everyone could see that a mile away.'

Noah groaned to himself. God, how embarrassing. He imagined all the adults having a good old chuckle about that, and his childish anger resurfaced. 'Don't be ridiculous,' he snapped. 'She was just a friend.'

'Sure she was,' the old man grinned annoyingly. 'And

I'm just a man who likes to catch the odd fish. How is she anyway? Any chance of a rekindled romance?' He asked hopefully.

'Not a chance,' he said firmly. 'Besides, she's married now.'

'What's the husband like?'

'No idea, she's here with her friend,' Noah told him, realising it was odd that the man wasn't around. 'She said to say hello to you by the way, and she will come and see you.' *When she put some clothes on,* his brain whispered flashing images of her without across his mind. Flustered, he straightened. 'I have to get on Mikiel. I might see you at the cafe later,' he said abruptly and pushed his way through the crowd of tourists cluttering up the aisles between the stalls. As he picked through the produce at Maria's stall of fresh fruits and vegetables from her garden, he pondered Belle's holidaying with a friend rather than her spouse. Maybe he would join them later, he thought. Sophia had said there might be other guests as the month went on.

To distract himself, he thought through the menu for lunch. He'd keep it simple with a lemon and garlic dressing, maybe some fresh chives and a salad with the robust, deep red tomatoes he'd just selected along with some rocket and cucumber, maybe some thinly sliced radish. He wouldn't have time to make bread, so he'd stop at the bakery on his way back to get some crusty rolls. After the lunch service, the afternoon would be stretched out in front of him, demanding to be filled.

He really should do some work on the house. The plaster he applied in the lounge would be more than dry by now, ready for painting. And he'd picked out the paint weeks ago, so there really was no excuse. Except… except the house had meant to have been for him and Sarah after they were married and when that didn't happen, he'd lost heart with the project. Friends had suggested he sell it, move on and start again somewhere else, but it had been a hard worked for gift from his grandparents and it would be disloyal to do anything but live there. With a sigh, he strapped his helmet on and climbed onto his bike. *One thing at a time, Noah, one thing at a time.*

Chapter Nine

Belinda had been joyfully reunited with her luggage and was unpacking it when Carla wandered into her room. 'How are you getting on, Hon?' she asked, plopping herself down on the bed.

'I'm nearly done,' Belinda told her, huffing at an errant curl that had fallen onto her face as she strained to put the last case on top of the wardrobe out of the way.

'Any news from the outside world? Have the kids said if they can come out yet?'

'Not yet, they're probably too busy. But never mind,' she said with a small smile that didn't reach her eyes.

'Well, they should make a bit of effort for their mom's birthday!' she said hotly. 'What are you gonna do after I leave? I don't like to think of your being lonely.'

Belinda laughed. 'I'll be fine, Cara. I'm used to my own company, and there are plenty of things to do here to keep me entertained.'

'I tell you what you could do to keep you entertained, that gorgeous chef. It's about time you got back in the saddle if you know what I mean,' she said with a salacious laugh.

Startled, Belinda spun round. 'What, Noah?'

'Yes, of course, Noah. How many gorgeous chefs do we have?'

'Don't be ridiculous,' she said hastily, turning back to put the neatly folded pile of tops and shorts in the dresser's drawer.

'There's nothing ridiculous about that man; it would do you the world of good after everything Mike put you through.'

'Carla, I'm really not ready to think about anything like that,' Belinda sighed, sitting down next to her friend. 'And besides,' she paused, biting her lower lip.

'Besides what?'

'Look, you may as well know. I know him, Noah I mean. From before, when I was a kid, when we used to holiday here.'

'Well, well, well. You kept that quiet, missy. I thought there was a strange friction between you two this morning. Didn't you like each other or something?'

'Quite the opposite; we were best friends when we were young. I've no idea why he's being so prickly with me now.'

'Well,' said Carla, getting to her feet. 'We'll just have to see what we can do to warm him up a bit!'

Later, as they were stretched out on the comfortable sunbeds by the pool, the cicadas droned lazily in the heat, and sunlight shimmered on the turquoise water. The air was thick with the scent of lemon and garlic drifting from the villa's open kitchen doors, an intoxicating promise of lunch and something far more elusive.

Belinda tilted her head slightly, the rim of her wide-brimmed hat shadowing her face, and watched Noah from behind her oversized sunglasses. He moved easily, without hesitation, the way people did when they were at home in their own skin. The boy she remembered, the one who'd once tripped over his own feet carrying a tray of lemonade, was gone. In his place was a man whose quiet confidence seemed to radiate from him in the same way sunlight danced off the pool tiles.

She watched as he unfolded linen napkins, the faintest smile touching his mouth when a breeze threatened to steal one away. His hands were capable, deliberate, the sort of hands that made her think of all the years that had passed between them. A pang of something old and familiar stirred inside her. Missing those summers with him had been more than nostalgia; it had been a loss she'd never quite managed to name. When her mother had moved them to America, she'd told herself it was an adventure, a chance to start fresh. But in quiet moments, she'd thought of this island, of the sea-salt air and Noah's uninhibited laughter, and felt a hollowness she could never explain to anyone, especially not to Mike.

Now, lying here again with the sound of Noah's footsteps soft on the patio stones, she wondered why she had let so many years slip away. Life had filled itself up, kept her busy. Marriage, children, charity events, polite dinners that blurred together, but not so completely that there hadn't been space for thoughts of what she'd left behind. *Not that busy*, she thought, her heart giving an unsteady beat.

And when Noah glanced her way, just for an instant before turning back to his task, Belinda felt a warmth that had nothing to do with the Maltese sun.

'Looks like lunch is nearly ready,' said Carla, sitting up, breaking into her reverie.

'Great, I'm famished. Although after that huge breakfast

I'll never know how.' Belinda stood and then stretched, before sliding her feet into her sandals and padding over to the table with Carla.

'This smells incredible,' she told Noah as he put the beautiful blue patterned plates down in front of them.

'Old family recipe,' he replied, setting a bowl of salad and some bread rolls on the table. 'Though I might've made a few improvements.'

She smiled faintly. 'You always did think you could improve everything.' He looked up at that, his eyes catching hers, and for an instant the years between them vanished.

'Maybe,' he said softly, 'but some things don't need improving.'

The remark hung there, light and harmless on the surface, but charged enough that Belinda had to look away first. She reached for the wine instead, filling her glass with something crisp and pale, and focused on the sound of the cicadas again, the gentle slap of pool water against the tiles, and tried to ignore the chuckles coming from Carla.

'Well, it looks like you and the hot chef have certainly got something cooking between you,' she said with a knowing grin as she took the wine bottle from her.

'I don't know what you're talking about,' Belinda said primly. Although she did. There had been something there, a frisson of heat in his eyes. Hadn't there? It was like he'd let his guard down, and the old Noah had surfaced.

Lunch was delicious. The simply cooked swordfish was bursting with lemon and garlic and a subtle hint of something she couldn't quite put her finger on, maybe capers, maybe just the sea itself. The tomatoes in the salad were impossibly sweet, their juices glistening in the afternoon light, mingling with the peppery bite of fresh basil and a drizzle of golden olive oil that shimmered like sunlight in a bottle. She had forgotten this as well, how wonderful everything tasted here, how the Maltese sun seemed to infuse every ingredient with life.

Carla leaned back in her chair with a contented sigh, swirling the last of her chilled white wine. 'You forget what real food tastes like,' she said, her voice warm and drowsy from the heat. 'Everything at home feels so... tired by comparison.'

Belinda smiled, nodding. 'It's true. Even the air tastes different.' She let her gaze drift over the terrace, where the vines twisted lazily around the wooden beams of the pergola, casting shifting patterns of shade across the tablecloth. Beyond the low stone wall, the sea stretched out in a blinding sheet of silver-blue, the horizon shimmering in the distance.

Carla reached for the bowl of olives, her bracelets catching the light. 'You seem lighter here,' she said casually, though her eyes were sharp with curiosity. 'Maybe it's just the sun, but I think this place suits you.'

Belinda laughed softly, though the sound caught in her throat. 'Maybe it's the wine,' she said, though both of them knew better. There was something about being back, the rhythm of the island, the taste of the food, the way memories lingered in the air, that was stirring things she thought she'd long buried.

Noah was all business when he returned to collect the debris of their lunch, barely looking at Belinda and giving a perfunctory nod of thanks when she thanked him for the delicious meal. *So much for the spark between them*, she thought after he'd wished them farewell after clearing up with promises of homemade croissants for breakfast the next day.

They lingered long after the plates were cleared with

another bottle of cold, crisp white wine, talking in the unhurried way only old friends could, about children and work and husbands, about the strange turns life had taken. Yet beneath their laughter, Belinda felt a quiet awareness humming through her, like the warmth radiating from the stone terrace beneath her bare feet. A sense of coming home, and of something waiting just beyond the edges of comfort.

Chapter Ten

When Noah pulled up in front of his house, he let the engine idle for a moment, taking in the sight of the squat little property nestled into the hillside. From here, the land fell away in gentle slopes toward the glittering sea; the light bounced off the waves in shifting bands of silver and blue. The house, built from the same pale Maltese limestone as the surrounding cliffs, seemed almost to grow out of the rock itself. In the late afternoon sun, the stone glowed with a honeyed warmth, holding the memory of the long, hot day.

He'd always loved how the place looked at this hour — solid, quiet, a little weathered but dignified. The surrounding land was still stubbornly bare, scrub and wild grasses pushing through the dust where he'd once imagined neat rows of vegetables and a riot of bougainvillea. His grand plans for a traditional garden had fallen away over time, just like so many other ambitions, set aside for later. Later had a way of stretching on indefinitely.

The small windows were shuttered tight against the heat, their cerulean paint a cheerful defiance against the muted stone. The same blue framed the front door, its colour slightly faded from the salt air, yet still vivid enough to catch the light and remind him why he'd chosen it. It was the colour of the sea on a perfect day, the colour of home.

He could almost imagine his grandmother sitting there again on the front steps, shelling peas into a bowl, humming softly under her breath. The thought made something twist gently in his chest. He exhaled, cut the engine, and listened for a moment to the sound of cicadas starting up in the dry grass, the faint rush of wind coming off the water.

It wasn't perfect, not by any measure. But as he climbed off the bike and walked toward the door, Noah felt that quiet pull again, the sense that this house, in its unpolished simplicity, was waiting for him to make it his. A sharp volley of barks greeted him as he pushed open the door, and Max, his rescue dog, leapt up to slather him with welcome-home licks.

'All right, boy, down you get,' he laughed at the mongrel. Max was an indeterminate mix of labrador, setter and probably a little bit of terrier thrown in. He'd been brought into the rescue centre where Noah volunteered four years ago. A tiny, shivering scrap that had been found in a bin on the outskirts of town, the thought of which still made his blood boil. It had been love at first sight, as after they'd cleaned the little pup, he'd curled up in a tight ball on Noah's lap and fallen into a deep, dreamless sleep as if he finally felt safe.

Once he was inside, the reflective mood that seeing Belle again seemed to have instilled in him continued, making him look around with fresh eyes. Inside, the air was cool and still, the thick limestone walls doing their part to hold back the heat. Noah paused in the doorway, letting his eyes adjust to the softer light. The faint scent of lemon oil and salt hung in the air, a mixture of his cleaning habits and the sea breeze that crept in no matter how tightly he shut the shutters.

The main room was simple, just as he'd intended when he'd started the renovation six years ago. The newly plastered, soon to be painted walls, their surface uneven from age, met a tiled floor of worn terracotta. A wide archway led to the kitchen, where the counters were smooth Maltese stone and the open shelves held a mismatched collection of crockery, some inherited from his family, some picked up from local markets on lazy Sunday mornings.

He walked through to the kitchen, Max trotting at his heels, and pulled open the shutters, flooding the room with light. It poured in like liquid gold, catching on the edges of the stone and turning the air itself to dust-flecked amber. From here, the view stretched all the way down to the sea. The horizon shimmered, blurring into the pale blue of the sky, and Noah stood for a long moment, resting a hand against the frame, feeling that familiar ache, the bittersweet comfort of belonging and loneliness intertwined.

Taking a deep breath, he walked into the narrow hallway, the familiar creak of the floorboards echoing softly in the stillness. The scent of old stone and sea air clung to the walls, faint but ever-present, like the island itself refused to let go of its memories. He paused at the door that had been shut for too long, its paint slightly cracked, the handle cool beneath his fingertips. It was strange how a simple door could hold so much of the past, as though time itself had gathered behind it, waiting for him to be ready.

He hesitated before turning the knob, knowing what lay beyond. The room that was meant to be theirs, the bedroom of the happy, newly married couple who never quite got to begin their life together. When he finally pushed it open, the hinges groaned in protest, releasing a faint puff of dust that drifted like ghostly mist through the shaft of afternoon light. Everything was as he remembered and yet utterly changed. The once-bright curtains were dulled with time, their edges stiff with dust. The grand four-poster bed dominated the room, its white canopy yellowed and still faintly scented with the lavender sachets Sarah had tucked between the sheets. And there, scattered across the coverlet, were the fragile remains of the rose petals he'd strewn that morning all those years ago, a surprise for her. Now they were brittle and curled, papery echoes of what had been soft and full of promise.

He moved closer, brushing his fingertips across the bedpost, tracing the faint grooves where sunlight and time had worn the varnish thin. A mirthless chuckle escaped him. 'Brittle, faded... much like me,' he murmured, his voice barely above a whisper. The words hung in the air, swallowed by the silence that seemed thicker in this room than anywhere else in the house.

The accident that day had taken so much, the laughter, the future they'd talked about in the lazy hours of summer afternoons, even his sense of direction for a while. He'd buried himself in work, in routine, in stone and sunlight, but grief had a way of settling into the bones, quiet and persistent. Standing there now, he felt the years folding in on themselves, the line between then and now blurring until all that was left was the ache of what might have been. He drew in another breath, letting the air fill his lungs, tasting dust and memory in equal measure.

He knew he would have to deal with it soon, open the shutters, strip the bed, let the light back in. But not today.

Not yet. Today, it was enough just to finally stand in the doorway, to remember her laughter in the hall, the echo of her footsteps, the way her hair had caught the sun.

He closed the door gently behind him, as though not to disturb what remained of her there, and stood for a long moment in the dim hallway, listening to the whisper of the sea outside. Seeing Belle after all these years had sparked something in him, like he was finally breathing again. Maybe he could start living rather than just existing. Maybe he could open his heart to the possibility of love again.

Chapter Eleven

After an incredibly idle afternoon that involved nothing more taxing than lazing around the pool, Belinda reading on her Kindle, Carla listening to her favourite podcasts, the women decided to get dressed up and take a wander into town for dinner. Sophia had sent a WhatsApp message to ask if they'd like her to book them somewhere exclusive, but Belinda wanted to leave it to chance and soak in the atmosphere of the old town and see where they ended up.

'That's not like you,' Carla had commented with an arched eyebrow, knowing her need to have everything organised to the nth degree. But Belinda had just shrugged. Her friend had been right; she was feeling lighter, free somehow, and it was quite liberating after years of orderliness. 'I'm trying to get into the holiday spirit,' was all she said in reply to the curious look.

The late afternoon sun bathed Valletta in liquid gold as Belinda and Carla made their way up one of the narrow limestone streets that wound toward the heart of the old town. The air shimmered with heat, and the sound of their sandals on the worn flagstones echoed faintly between the tall façades that leaned close together like old friends sharing secrets. Everywhere, the warm stone glowed, and the faint smell of the sea drifted through the air, carried by a lazy breeze from the Grand Harbour.

They passed beneath balconies painted in shades of faded turquoise and jade, their shutters slightly askew, potted geraniums spilling colour over the railings. Laundry flapped lazily above their heads, the scent of soap mingling with frying onions and car exhaust, a domestic symphony that somehow felt comforting. Every so often, a church bell rang out, its solemn tone bouncing down the hill, mingling with the chatter from nearby shops and the laughter of children chasing a ball across the street.

Carla tilted her face toward the sky, shading her eyes with one hand as she turned slowly in a little piazza. 'It's even more beautiful than I imagined,' she said, her voice full of wonder. 'It feels like stepping into another time. Every street looks like a painting.'

Belinda smiled, watching her friend take it all in. 'It does that to you,' she said softly. 'There's something about Valletta, the colours, the air, even the light. It hasn't really changed since I was a child.'

'Is it strange for you?' Carla asked after a moment. 'Coming back after all these years?'

Belinda hesitated, her gaze following a pigeon that fluttered across the square. 'Yes. I used to spend every summer here when I was a kid. My grandparents had a little place nearby. Those summers felt endless, sunburned afternoons, swimming until my fingers wrinkled, and evenings sitting outside listening to the cicadas.' She smiled faintly, lost in the recollection. 'And of course Noah actually liked me then!'

'Oh, that man still likes you, honey, as sure as eggs are eggs. The way he looks at you when he thinks you're not looking? Phew,' she fanned her face with exaggerated hand movements and rolled her eyes dramatically.

'He does not!' Belinda shoved her friend playfully, feeling every bit like a teenager again. 'Come on, let's find something to eat.'

They found a simple trattoria, tucked away down a tiny cobbled alley, and shared a selection of starters and a salad. Even though lunch had been light, they were both still sated and couldn't make room for any heavy pasta dishes, no matter how delicious they sounded. 'We'll have to come back when we have more appetite,' Belinda said, wiping her mouth with a linen napkin and sitting back with a satisfied air. Carla nodded in agreement.

'I'm going to be the size of my house by the time I get back; I'll have to move.'

Belinda laughed at this; they both knew that Carla was one of those annoying people who could eat like a horse and never put on an ounce. They decided to walk back along the harbour front to burn at least a few calories before returning to the villa. The sun had disappeared, but it was still warm, the streets alive with families taking a stroll and people collecting at the open-air cafes that were dotted along the front. The atmosphere was vibrant and full of chatter and laughter.

Belinda suddenly stopped, staring at a small cafe on the next corner, full of old men arguing loudly but with good spirits, as if they were enjoying the debate. The faded green awning and the ancient wooden tables were exactly as she remembered. 'Good grief, Franko's is still there.'

'What's Franko's?' Carla queried, seeing nothing exciting about the tiny establishment.

'It's where the old guys from the Boċċi teams congregate and argue about who's the best,' she replied, a wide smile lighting up her face. 'And I think I know who's making the most noise. Come on.'

Before Carla had the chance to ask what the hell Boċċi was, Belinda grabbed her arm and dragged her towards the cafe. As they approached the entirely male clientele seated at the small wooden tables, a silence descended as they noticed the interlopers. Carla felt deeply uncomfortable under their scrutiny, but Belinda was beaming like a child on Christmas morning that had just seen their pile of presents. A small, wizened old man, who had obviously never heard of SPF given his walnut-shaded and wrinkled skin, slowly pushed his chair back and stood. 'Anġlu, you are here!'

'Yes, Mikiel. I came back,' Belinda answered simply, before being embraced in a bear-like hug that took her breath away. When he eventually released her, Mikiel shooed away the others at his table and insisted they sat down for a glass of Lumincetta. Introductions were made, and the old man wasted no time grilling Belinda about her life over the decades since he last saw her, in that unabashed way his generation did.

'So, you're married, Noah tells me.'

Taken aback, Belinda took a moment to sip the sweet yet sour, pale-yellow liquid in her glass. 'I was,' she said with a dip of her head. 'Not anymore.'

'Interesting,' he murmured with a delighted smile. 'And how was it seeing young Noah again?' he asked with a mischievous grin.

'Um,' she hesitated. 'Okay, I guess. He's changed though; he's not how I remember him.'

'Hardly surprising after what happened,' Mikiel said, his features darkening for a moment.

Carla, who'd been sitting back enjoying watching the interaction, leant forward, her instincts telling her that this was something her friend needed to know.

And she was right.

Chapter Twelve

Noah was at the villa early to egg-wash the croissants he'd prepared the day before and left to proof overnight in the fridge. With music in his ears, and in the kitchen, his safe space, he felt happier than he had in a long time. Even the thought of seeing Belle didn't feel quite so daunting, despite the weird friction between them yesterday. The fact that she'd remembered, or even noticed for that matter, his boyish attempts to improve everything they did had startled him. He'd felt a strange sense of connection with her in that moment, and if he was honest, if her friend hadn't been leering at him knowingly, he might have sat down and explored that feeling with her. He shook these thoughts away as he moved through the small space on instinct, the sizzle of olive oil as he fried peppers for the omelets, the low bubbling of coffee in the machine, the soft scrape of a knife against bread. Simple, grounding things. Things that didn't ask much of him. He didn't hear her at first, not over the hiss of the pan and the sound in his ears. But something in the air shifted, the faint rustle of movement behind him, the light tread of bare feet on tile and before she even spoke, he knew.

He turned slightly, spatula still in hand, and there she was, framed in the doorway, the sunlight behind her making her hair glow. Older, of course, but unmistakable. The same steadiness in her eyes, the same quiet way she seemed to fill a room without trying. For a heartbeat, he couldn't say a word. 'You're up early,' he managed, stopping the music and turning back to the stove so she wouldn't see the sudden rush of memory across his face.

'I smelled breakfast,' she said, a hint of a smile in her voice. 'Couldn't resist the croissants.'

He nodded toward the counter, reaching for the coffeepot. 'Help yourself. It's fresh.' When she came to pour herself a cup, her sleeve brushed his arm, a light touch, fleeting but enough to make him still. He hadn't realised how long it had been since someone had stood this close. For a while, they said nothing, just the indistinct murmur of the stove between them.

Then, quietly, she said, 'I didn't know. About Sarah and your dad. I'm so sorry, Noah.'

His hand froze, the spatula halfway to the plate. He set it down carefully, aware of how even silence could carry weight. 'Most people don't,' he said finally. 'It was a long time ago. How do you...?'

'Mikiel,' she said with a smile. 'I bumped into him last night.'

He could feel her gaze on him, gentle, searching, and he wondered what she saw now. The same boy who used to race her to the cliffs each morning, or the man who'd spent years learning how to live with these ghosts. He didn't need anybody's sympathy, especially not Belle's. 'You can take your coffee out to the terrace; breakfast service isn't for another half hour.'

He saw a flash of pain in her eyes, then her face stiffened with something like anger. 'Good to know,' she said curtly before stomping out of the kitchen. Noah turned back to the stove, a frown tugging at his mouth. It was going to be a long morning.

Serving breakfast was an uncomfortable affair. He knew they were talking about him, about the awful thing that had happened, by the silence that descended every time he appeared with a platter of fruit or a top up of coffee. Noah could have kissed Sophia when she arrived, bustling in with chatter and ideas of excursions to fill in the silence. 'I'm not sure about horse riding,' Carla was saying as he came to clear the table. 'It would be a bit of a busman's holiday for me. But I do like the sound of a day out on a fancy boat.'

'Can we wait until next week to do that?' Belinda asked suddenly, looking up from her phone with a big smile. 'It looks like Jason is coming out for a few days!'

'Big of him to take out from his busy schedule,' said Carla snarkily. She loved her friends' kids but felt they could have been so much more supportive of their mother these last months. Noah had been on his way back to the kitchen but wheeled around.

'Is that your husband?' he asked Belle in what he hoped was an even tone, despite the unpleasant spike to his heart rate. Carla jumped in before Belinda had time to wipe the look of surprise off her face.

'No honey. Belinda's not married anymore; she just hasn't got around to changing her name on any paperwork for some unknown reason,' she said, looking pointedly at her friend.

'Jason is my son,' she told him, with a curious look on her face as she gazed at him.

'Oh, I see,' he said with a cough and hurried back inside, wondering why the news that Belle was no longer married affected him so much. He busied himself rinsing dishes and stacking the dishwasher in the precise manner he always did that would drive some people crazy. His phone chimed, and he dug it out of his apron pocket to see a message from Mikiel reminding him that tomorrow was the big Boċċi game and if Noah missed it Mikiel would personally curse him and all of his descendants. Chuckling to himself, he returned to the terrace to discuss whether they would like lunch or dinner.

Sophia was just collecting herself to leave, saying, 'I'll get your driver to pick you up at twelve o'clock. It's only a twenty-minute drive to Mdina.'

'That sounds perfect,' Belinda replied with a smile, which dropped a little when she saw Noah. 'Carla, why don't you have a chat with our chef about dinner tonight?'

Carla stared her down. 'Oh, I think you should have that conversation.'

Belinda stood up, picking her phone up from the table. 'You go ahead; I have some emails to answer,' she said intractably and stalked across the terrace, disappearing through the open french doors.

Chapter Thirteen

In the sanctuary of her bedroom, Belinda sank down onto her bed and thought through her conversation with Noah. She had genuinely wanted to offer condolences; how could she not? To lose your wife to be and your father in a pointless car crash on your wedding day was a complete horror story made flesh. She remembered Bastjan's much-loved Morris Minor that he cleaned religiously every Sunday until its sky-blue paintwork shone. He always said it was more reliable than any woman and never let him down. But that day it had, its breaks failing as he was driving the bride to church, forcing them through a barrier into the valley below. Their deaths had been instant; Mikiel had told her with a sorrowful smile. The only saving grace in the dreadful situation. Belinda felt a shiver ripple through her, despite the heat of the day. No wonder Noah seemed so miserable; it was understandable. Something like that would be almost impossible to recover from. It didn't quite explain his reaction to her, though; she thought with a frown furrowing her brow.

After a quick shower, Belinda pulled on one of her favourite new sundresses. It was lightweight, with a fitted bodice and flared hemline that made her feel womanly. The deep blue, dotted with tiny flowers that made her smile. She had revamped her wardrobe since her divorce, picking things she loved rather than things that would be suitable for corporate events and dinners. That reminded her she'd seen a voicemail from Mike; it was probably best to listen in case it was important. He'd been sending messages daily, which was unlike him, even when they were married.

'Belinda, why aren't you answering my messages?' His angry tone immediately put her hackles up. But then his voice softened. 'Look, I know I've been… well, I know I behaved awfully. But the thing is, the thing is I think I've made a mistake. Can we talk?'

Stunned, Belinda threw her phone on the bed, as if touching it was connecting her to him in some way. What on earth did Mike think was going to happen? A bit of soft-soaping, maybe some flowers and a few dinners and she would forgive the years of lies and deceit? He really was unbelievable, she thought angrily as she laced up her grecian sandals, almost cutting off the blood supply to her feet. She took a couple of calming breaths, loosened the laces, then headed back downstairs to tell Carla this latest development.

'He said what?' Carla screeched predictably, pacing the terrace. 'That no good, son of a bitch thinks you would even consider looking at him again? And what about that poor girl he'd shacked up with? She must be nearly due by now!'

'I know,' Belinda said with a shrug. 'It's insane.'

'I hope you told him where to get off,' she replied, cracking her knuckles menacingly.

Smiling at her friend's anger on her behalf, Belinda said, 'I didn't respond. Nor do I intend to. The only time I ever plan to be in the same vicinity as that man is if either of the kids gets married and I have to be. I've told them both I'd be quite happy if they eloped!'

This seemed to placate her a little, so Belinda carried on. 'Anyway, go and get yourself dressed; there's only half an hour or so until we're picked up to visit the vineyard.'

The minivan hummed softly as it pulled away from Valletta, gliding through the sun-washed streets that gave way to the open Maltese countryside. Carla sank back into the cream leather seat with a contented sigh, her sunglasses perched low on her nose. 'Now this,' she said, grinning, 'is how to travel.

Belinda smiled, turning her gaze to the window. The city's limestone walls soon fell behind them, replaced by rolling hills scattered with olive groves and wild thyme. The air outside shimmered with heat, blurring the edges of distant stone farmhouses. Every so often, the driver slowed to let a truck of melons pass, the sweet scent of fruit briefly drifting through the open vents.

They wound their way inland, the Mediterranean glittering faintly to their left, the landscape flattening into terraced fields bordered by dry stone walls. Belinda watched as the familiar ochre tones deepened in the afternoon sun, this land she'd once known by heart and had somehow forgotten how to belong to. She felt a twinge of nostalgia, a longing that was both comforting and sad. Carla leaned over to point out a tiny chapel perched on a rise. 'Everything here feels like it's been standing for centuries,' she said. 'It all feels so old.'

'Older than both of us put together,' Belinda murmured, her lips curving into a smile.

As they climbed toward Mdina, the "Silent City" came into view, its honey-coloured ramparts glowing softly against the sky. Beyond it, the vineyard spread across the hillside in neat, sun-drenched rows, the leaves trembling in the warm breeze. The scent of crushed earth and ripening grapes met them as the driver turned into a gravel lane lined with cypress trees.

Carla exhaled with delight. 'Wine and views. What more could we possibly need?'

Belinda smiled again, though her thoughts drifted elsewhere, to memory, to Noah, and to the quiet ache of returning home.

Chapter Fourteen

Noah had been home to take Max for a walk, to clear his head and think through the meal that Carla had insisted on for this evening without even glancing at the choices in his folder. They made their way through the familiar landscape, Max bounding on ahead and then stopping to check he was there now and then, Noah taking in a deep lungful of the salt-tainted air. Oysters to start, followed by salmon with asparagus and then strawberries dipped in dark chocolate for dessert. It was the kind of meal he'd make for a romantic rendezvous, not an obvious meal for two friends on holiday. Mentally shrugging away that thought, he planned his shopping and, more importantly, exactly what he was going to say to Mikiel for blabbing his life story to Belle.

'I need a word with you, old man,' he said without preamble when Mikiel had finished serving his previous customer.

'I am a good person to talk to; I am very wise,' he

grinned as he rearranged the display of today's catch, which looked to be bountiful.

'Why did you tell Belle about what happened?' He didn't need to say about what, there was only one thing that had happened in his life that people seemed to remember.

'Why would I not?' the old man shrugged. 'It happened, you were deeply affected by it, and she seemed concerned.'

Noah looked at him sharply. He'd been going to say it wasn't anyone's damn business but his own, but instead the words 'Belle was concerned about me?' shot out of his mouth, his heart doing a weird skippy thing in his chest.

Mikiel laughed. 'Yes, boy. She was, and I can't think of a better person for you to talk it through with, given that you won't talk to anyone else about it.'

'There's nothing to talk about. It happened, it's over, and I'm getting on with my life!'

'If you say so,' he replied obliquely. 'Now, are you just here to shout at me or are you here to purchase some of my fine fish?'

Noah knew there was no point in trying to reason with his old friend, so reeled off his order for today. But his mind was elsewhere. Did Belle actually have any vestiges of feelings for him? He'd always assumed she hadn't given him a second thought. After all, there's been no letters, no attempts to revisit until now, and the fact that he worked at the villa was incidental; there wouldn't have been a reconnection otherwise, he was sure.

Back at the villa, Noah moved with quiet precision through the sunlit kitchen, every motion deliberate and unhurried. The wide wooden counter was laid with the simple luxury of the morning's catch: oysters glistening on crushed ice, thin slices of salmon cured with salt and lemon, and a bundle of tender asparagus waiting to be blanched to a perfect green. The air was filled with the clean, briny scent of the sea, the faint citrus of the marinade, and the deeper, bittersweet perfume of melted dark chocolate that he was stirring gently over low heat. He dipped each strawberry with care, letting the glossy coating cling and set before placing it on the tray beside him. Sunlight filtered through the open shutters, catching in the sheen of the oysters and the slow curl of steam from the pan. And though he worked alone, the villa didn't feel empty; it pulsed with the easy heartbeat of routine, of creation, and, somewhere deep beneath it all, the faint anticipation of serving it to someone who might understand.

He heard them long before he saw them. The villa, usually calm in the late afternoon, suddenly filled with laughter, loud, rolling, and completely unrestrained. The sound of shoes clattering across the tiles was followed by the unmistakable crash of something small (hopefully not breakable). Noah paused mid-chop, smiling despite himself. They'd clearly enjoyed the wine tasting.

A moment later, Carla burst through the doorway, holding a box of wine like it was an ancient relic that might disappear if she blinked. Her hair was slightly windswept, her lipstick a little smudged, and she was radiating triumph. 'Tadaah!' she announced grandly, nearly tripping over her own feet as she reached the counter. She placed the box down with both hands and an expression of intense concentration. 'We brought wine,' she said, nodding gravely, as if delivering a royal decree.

Noah glanced toward the corner, where a fully stocked wine fridge and a floor-to-ceiling rack gleamed. 'We do have quite a lot of wine already,' he said mildly, fighting back a grin.

'Ah,' Carla said, pointing one finger upward like a

philosopher about to make a grand revelation, 'but this is special wine.'

'Special wine,' he echoed. 'Of course.'

'The man… What was his name, Belinda?' she asked over her shoulder.

'Zachary,' came the reply. Belinda strolled into the kitchen, calm and composed in contrast to Carla's theatrical entrance. Her cheeks were flushed, her hair a little tousled, and her eyes, dark and bright with amusement, met Noah's across the room. 'And Zachary,' she continued, 'was very good looking and somehow managed to convince my dear friend here that we needed to spend a couple of hundred dollars on his special wine.'

Carla nodded vigorously. 'He had dimples, Noah. Dimples! You can't say no to dimples.'

Noah chuckled, pretending to think. 'Ah, I see. Well then, if the dimples endorsed it, we'd best serve it with dinner.'

Belinda laughed, the sound soft but rich, and he couldn't help grinning back. For a fleeting moment, amid the scent of garlic and the chaos of their arrival, he thought he felt a little more alive than he had in years.

Chapter Fifteen

By the time dinner was ready, Carla was serenading the wine bottles. Or at least, that's what it looked like to Belinda, who was trying very hard not to laugh as her friend hummed dramatically while reading the label aloud in her best "posh sommelier" voice.

Noah, ever patient, plated up food as though nothing was amiss, cool, steady, maddeningly composed. Belinda couldn't help but notice how he moved around, all calm efficiency and quiet confidence, completely unfazed by Carla's antics. The years had settled into him well; his shoulders broader, his features more defined. Even his laugh lines suited him. It was deeply unfair, really.

Carla poured the "special" wine with grand ceremony, managing to slosh a good portion onto the tablecloth. 'Oops,' she said cheerfully. 'Extra flavour for the table!'

'Please tell me it's not red,' Noah murmured, rescuing the bottle from her grip.

'Pink!' Carla declared proudly, as if that somehow justified everything.

Belinda bit her lip to keep from laughing. 'She means rosé,' she said helpfully, taking her own glass.

Noah poured for her with a quiet smile. 'Pink, right. A connoisseur's choice.'

When he handed her the glass, his fingers brushed hers. The touch was fleeting, almost accidental, but it sent a tiny pulse of warmth through her. She looked up, half expecting him to glance away, but his gaze lingered, steady, unreadable, and a little too knowing.

Carla raised her glass high. 'To new friends, old flames, and expensive mistakes!'

'Which category does the wine fall into?' Noah asked dryly.

'All three,' Belinda said before she could stop herself. He laughed then, an honest, deep laugh that filled the air and made her heart skip just a little.

Dinner was delicious, though Belinda barely tasted it. Between the wine, the teasing, and the way Noah's eyes kept finding hers across the table, she felt light and unmoored. The years between them seemed to fade with every shared glance, every easy exchange. When the last of the "special" wine was gone and Carla was happily declaring she'd "help with dishes tomorrow," Belinda found herself lingering as Noah cleared the plates.

'Thanks for dinner,' she said softly. 'It was… perfect.'

He looked up from the sink, with that familiar half-smile tugging at his mouth. 'It's good to have your company again.'

Something unspoken stretched between them then, warm and uncertain, like the last glow of sunset through the open shutters. And for the first time, Belinda wondered if maybe, just maybe, she'd come back to Malta for more than nostalgia.

The next morning, Belinda woke surprisingly early and took a moment to luxuriate in the wonderfully comfortable bed. It seemed like the mattress cradled her, the linen soft against her skin, still faintly scented with lavender from the villa's laundry cupboard. The sun, already bright and unashamedly enthusiastic for the day, filtered through the half-open shutters, casting soft golden ripples across the wardrobe, the tiled floor, her outstretched legs.

She stretched like a cat, her muscles pleasantly heavy, and let herself enjoy the rare sensation of waking without an alarm, without demands, without Mike's clipped voice dictating a schedule. Just light, warmth, and quiet. Then she remembered Carla's antics of the night before. Belinda huffed a laugh into her pillow. The wine, the singing and the dramatic declaration that she was "emotionally bonded" to Zachary, the handsome winemaker. Yes, Carla wouldn't be emerging from her room until at least lunchtime. Possibly later if she'd discovered the blackout curtains. But the warm amusement in her chest shifted as another memory surfaced. Noah.

The way he'd looked at her last night as he topped up her glass, his eyes catching the light like the sea at dusk. The way he'd laughed, really laughed, for the first time since she'd arrived, as though something inside him had loosened. And the way her whole body had responded, traitorously, to the slightest accidental brush of his fingers. A spark. A fizz low in her stomach that had no business being there. She pressed a hand over her eyes, trying, and failing, to slow the flutter of her heartbeat.

What was she doing?

He was Noah. Her childhood partner-in-crime. The boy who taught her to whistle through her fingers and dared her to climb the fig tree behind the old fort. The man who had lost so much and built walls around every tender place. And yet…

Her mind drifted back to the kitchen, to the warmth in his eyes, to the way the corners of his mouth had lifted when he caught her watching him. There had been something there, familiar but new, unsteady but hopeful. Belinda exhaled slowly, pushing the covers aside. If she stayed in bed thinking about it, she might drive herself mad. Coffee. She needed coffee. And maybe she'd find Noah in the kitchen again, sleeves rolled up, hair mussed from sleep, sunlight catching on the quiet strength of his arms as he cooked. The thought sent another warm flutter through her. 'Get a grip, Belle,' she whispered to herself, tying her robe. But even as she said it, she was already moving toward the door.

Belinda padded quietly down the hallway, trying to look composed despite the ridiculous amount of internal pep-talking she'd done on the walk from her room. It was just breakfast. Just Noah. She absolutely wasn't hoping he'd be standing at the stove looking annoyingly attractive in the morning light. She walked through the door to the kitchen, and nearly burst out laughing.

Noah was indeed at the stove… but he was also locked in a staring contest with a small, determined gecko perched on the rim of the fruit bowl on the counter. He held a wooden spoon in one hand, mid-stir, while the gecko glared at him like it had a personal vendetta.

'Please tell me you're not negotiating with wildlife,' Belinda said.

He startled, turning toward her with a sheepish look. 'It's not negotiation,' he said, nodding toward the creature. 'It's intimidation.' The gecko blinked lazily, unimpressed.

Belinda snorted. 'Looks like it's winning.'

'It usually does,' Noah muttered, slowly sliding an orange from the bowl. 'This is the third time this week.'

Belinda leaned against the counter, laughter warming her chest. 'Well, at least it's cute.'

Noah gave her a look. 'That thing jumped on my shoulder yesterday. Cute is not the word I'd use.'

'Sounds traumatic,' she said lightly. 'Should I call someone?'

He narrowed his eyes in mock offense. 'Are you teasing me before coffee?'

'Always.'

A smile tugged at his lips, the soft, rare kind that made her stomach do something far too dramatic for this early in the day.

'You're up early,' he said, turning back to the pan. 'Thought you'd sleep in after last night.'

'Carla will,' Belinda said, opening a cupboard to retrieve a mug and pretending she wasn't hyper-aware of him. 'Possibly until Thursday.'

'Should I check she's still breathing?'

'She's fine. She said, "if I die, I want to be buried with the rosé."'

Noah paused. 'The "special" wine?'

'The very one.'

He laughed. Low, warm, the kind of sound that made the whole kitchen feel brighter. And God help her, she realised she wanted to hear it again. Wanted to see his eyes crinkle at the corners. Wanted… well, she would not think too hard about that part yet.

'Breakfast?' he asked, plating eggs with far too much casual grace for a man who'd just lost a fight with a gecko.

'Yes, please,' she replied. 'And maybe later, you can give

me a tour of the villa. Show me all your… wildlife challenges.'

He shot her a sideways look, amused. 'Only if you promise not to laugh.'

Belinda smiled sweetly. 'I promise nothing.'

And as he handed her the plate, his fingers brushing hers just a fraction longer than necessary, she realised something undeniable: She was in trouble.

The nice, long-forgotten, heart-thumping kind of trouble.

Chapter Sixteen

Noah carried the last plate out onto the terrace, the morning sun already warming the stone, the sea stretching out like a sheet of soft blue silk below. He set down the rest of the eggs, the grilled tomatoes, the fresh bread he'd baked at dawn, and tried not to think about the way Belle's laughter from the kitchen still echoed faintly in his ears. She was seated at the table now, legs tucked beneath her, hair gathered in a loose tie that made her look effortlessly beautiful in a way she probably didn't realise she possessed. She caught his eye as he placed a bowl of fruit down; her smile soft and knowing, and he felt that stupid flutter in his chest again.

Ridiculous, really. He was a grown man. He had survived kitchen fires, demanding wedding parties, and a gecko with boundary issues. There was no way he should not be undone by a smile. Noah had just set the coffeepot down when a noise came from inside the villa. A groan. A low, theatrical groan, the kind reserved for soap operas and the deeply hungover.

'Brace yourself,' Belinda murmured, hiding a grin behind her mug. A moment later, Carla appeared in the doorway. Or rather, hovered. With one hand gripping the doorframe for balance, the other shielding her eyes as though the Mediterranean sun were personally betraying her.

'Oh God,' she croaked. 'Why is it so bright?'

Belinda choked on her coffee. Noah pressed his lips together to keep from laughing. Carla took a tentative step forward, wobbling slightly.

'And why does my tongue feel… furry? Did I eat a carpet?'

'You drank several glasses of rosé,' Belinda said helpfully.

'Special rosé,' Noah added.

Carla winced. 'Don't say the word "special" to me ever again. My wallet is still traumatised.'

She reached the table and collapsed into a chair with all the grace of a Victorian heroine succumbing to consumption. From this angle, Noah wasn't entirely convinced she wouldn't slide right off onto the terrace tiles. 'I need water,' she whispered. 'Preferably blessed by a priest if the pool boy is about.'

Belinda was shaking with suppressed laughter now. Noah handed Carla a glass, which she accepted with tragic gratitude, taking slow sips like it was the elixir of life.

'Did I embarrass myself yesterday?' she asked finally, peeking over the rim.

'Yes,' Belinda and Noah said in unison.

Carla blinked. 'Excellent. Means I had fun.'

Noah chuckled, turning back to the table to set down the last of the breakfast dishes. As he did, he caught Belinda watching him, chin resting in her hand, eyes warm and amused. When their gazes met, something in his chest loosened. Despite the chaos, despite Carla's groaning, despite the lingering weight of old memories, this morning he felt good.

Alive.

And as he watched Belinda reach for her fork, sunlight catching in her hair, he realised, with a quiet certainty, that he was looking forward to whatever came next.

'So, did you get it on with the hot chef after I went to bed?' he heard Carla ask in a stage whisper. He paused inside the door, out of sight, intrigued.

'No, I did not!' Belle answered, sounding affronted. 'Why would you think that? And why do you suddenly sound less hungover?' She asked suspiciously.

Carla gave a bark of laughter that carried easily into the villa. 'Why do you think I ordered all that aphrodisiac food for dinner and then skulked off early? I wasn't nearly as tipsy as you think. I should have been an actress,' she declared. There was a long pause. He could imagine the look on Belle's face, and he grinned, at least he knew why the oysters were on the menu now.

'Carla Jackson, you are a devious minx,' Belle retorted. 'Keep your matchmaking machinations out of my love life, or lack of one. Do you hear?'

Carla laughed again. 'I hear you, Belinda, no need to get all uppity.'

Noah startled as Sophia appeared by his side and looked at him quizzically. 'Everything okay, chef?'

'Yup, yup. Just off to the kitchen to grab some more bread,' he said hurriedly, aware that the conversation had halted outside, and scuttled off. The concierge reappeared in the kitchen a short while later, writing some notes on her clipboard. She looked up at him.

'They're not planning to go far today, and they'd like dinner service again, please. You can choose the menu, apparently.'

'Excellent,' he replied, relieved. He'd been worried they'd ask for lunch, which would have prevented him getting to the start of the Boċċi match and he'd have to face the wrath of Mikiel, who took such things seriously indeed. 'Thanks, Sophia, see you tomorrow,' he said as she walked to the back door.

Noah mentally ran through his day. He could finish clearing up, pop home for a quick shower and collect Max before going to the game. His dog loved the attention he received at the gatherings, although he'd have to keep him on a lead to stop him chasing the balls. And then he could come back to the villa and cook for Belle again. His face broke out in a broad smile. It was going to be a good day.

Chapter Seventeen

'I hope you're happy now,' Belinda said hotly when Sophia left. 'Noah obviously just heard all about your romantic plans for us. It's so embarrassing.' Carla just gave an impish grin from behind her coffee mug. 'And anyway, why am I being subjected to this ridiculous plan? Why aren't you looking for a man? You've been single a lot longer than I have.'

'Hank left very big boots to fill, if you know what I mean,' she replied with a waggle of her perfectly sculpted eyebrows.

Belinda huffed out a breath in consternation, but couldn't restrain the smile that broke out. Carla might be exasperating at times, but she was always good company. 'What do you want to do today? Shall we go shopping in the Old Town?' Belinda asked.

'God, no! I may not have been as drunk as I appeared yesterday, but I still need a few hours to recover before I do anything complicated like getting dressed. And don't forget you promised that old man who looks like a prune we'd go to his bocky game this afternoon.'

'I think you mean Boċċi,' said Belinda, still smiling as she glanced at her watch. 'That gives you about three hours to get yourself together. Do you think you can manage that?'

The small pitch behind Franko's café was filled with serious old men and an air of expectation. Belinda tried to explain the importance of the game of boċċi in Malta, and a little of the rules as she remembered.

'So, the aim is… to throw the big ball close to the little ball?' Carla asked, squinting at the sandy pitch as though expecting enlightenment to rise from it.

'Yes,' Belinda said patiently, 'but with skill.'

Carla nodded solemnly. 'Skill. Right. Got it. Looks like pétanque.'

Three Maltese men turned their heads in unison and gave her matching looks of deep offense. Belinda elbowed her. 'Don't say pétanque here unless you want to start an international incident.'

Carla whispered, 'how was I supposed to know? They're just throwing balls.' Another man glared at her. Belinda gently clamped a hand over her friend's mouth.

'Shhh. Be respectful. They take this very seriously. My grandfather used to spend entire afternoons here. If anyone so much as sneezed during his throw, he'd talk about it for a week.'

They watched as a wiry man with a shock of white hair stepped forward, the crowd, well, the seven old men, holding their breath. He swung his arm with a flourish and sent the ball arcing through the air with deceptive grace.

When it landed precisely where he wanted, the men erupted in low murmurs of approval. Carla blinked. 'Oh wow. That… was actually impressive.'

The man closest to them puffed up proudly, clearly having overheard. 'Dan hu l-kaptan tal-pitch,' he declared. The captain of the pitch.

Belinda smiled. 'See? Told you. National sport.'

Carla leaned closer, fascinated now. 'Do they have trophies? Leagues? Trading cards?'

'Carla…'

'Oh my God, Belinda, imagine! A boċċi sticker book.'

Belinda snorted, earning them yet another pair of scandalized looks. They edged over to sit at one of Franko's mismatched wooden tables, sipping on a cold Kinnie Franko insisted they try. The bittersweet drink fizzed on their tongues as the game resumed with renewed intensity.

Carla tapped her chin thoughtfully. 'You know… this actually looks fun. Kind of meditative. Relaxing, even.' At that precise moment, two players burst into a heated argument in Maltese, complete with wild hand gestures and accusations that sounded like someone was being personally attacked on a molecular level. Belinda raised an eyebrow.

Carla whispered, 'Perhaps… less relaxing than I thought.'

Belinda grinned into her drink. 'Welcome to Malta.'

Just then, Franko himself shuffled out of the café carrying two plates of ħobż biż-żejt, placing them on their table with a wink. 'Eat, eat. The game gets better on a full stomach.'

Carla beamed. 'Everything does.'

And as Belinda took a bite, the taste of ripe tomatoes, olive oil, and childhood summers washing over her, she realised how good it felt to be exactly here, sun on her skin,

Carla beside her, Noah somewhere in the back of her thoughts like a soft, persistent glow. As if her thoughts had conjured him, Carla suddenly nudged Belinda hard enough to nearly spill her Kinnie.

'Belinda, look what the cat dragged in. Or should I say the dog?'

Belinda followed her gaze and felt something warm and unsettling spark in her chest. Noah stood at the far side of the pitch, the dog trotting proudly beside him as if he owned the entire operation. The sun lit Noah from behind, catching in his hair and the broad line of his shoulders as he laughed at something Mikiel was saying. He looked relaxed. Happier than she'd seen him since she'd arrived. It did things to her heart she wasn't ready to deal with. Max spotted her first. His ears shot up. His tail started windmilling. Then, like a missile propelled by pure enthusiasm, he launched himself across the pitch.

'No, no, no, Max—MAX!' Noah called, breaking into a jog. Too late. Max skidded onto the pitch mid-play, sending pebbles flying, and every man over sixty reacted with the same scandalised gasp.

Carla stage-whispered, 'Belinda, your boyfriend's dog is causing havoc.'

Belinda spluttered, 'he is not my—Max! Off the pitch!' she added, having gathered the dog's name. Mikiel boomed with laughter; arms folded over his chest.

'Just like old times! Noah causing trouble, Belinda cleaning it up!'

Belinda covered her face with one hand. 'Mikiel, you are not helping.' Max finally reached her, planting both paws on her knees and demanding adoration. She complied, honestly; who could resist? Before glancing up just as Noah reached them. He looked breathless, apologetic and unfairly attractive in the morning sun.

'Sorry,' he said, trying to wrangle Max, who was now leaning completely against Belinda like he'd found his soulmate. 'He saw someone he likes, apparently.' Belinda felt a warm flutter at that. Carla, of course, ruined the moment.

'Same, buddy. Happens to the best of us.'

Noah shot her a look; she winked. Belinda wished briefly for an invisibility cloak. Mikiel strode over, arms wide. 'Belle, you brought good luck! Our captain's throw nearly beat Gianni's!'

Carla nodded sagely. 'We're very supportive. Mostly because we don't understand what's happening.'

Mikiel clapped Noah on the back. 'You staying for the match? Stay. We need Belle's cheering. And your dog's chaos. The other team is terrified now.' Noah's eyes found Belinda's. Warm and quiet. With that gentle spark she'd been trying not to think about.

'If Belle's staying,' he said softly, 'I'll stay.'

Her breath caught. Mikiel didn't notice, already shouting instructions at his team. Carla did notice, however, and made a sound that was dangerously close to a squeal. Belinda scratched Max's ears to cover her blush. And as the game resumed with fresh intensity, Noah stood beside her, Max leaning happily against her leg, and the Maltese sun warming everything around them, Belinda realised she couldn't remember the last time she felt this content.

Chapter Eighteen

The post-match celebrations were even more heated than the game itself, a glorious symphony of passionate bickering and exaggerated retellings of throws that would have put Olympic athletes to shame. The tables at Franko's café had been dragged together until they formed one long, wobbly surface, and now both teams crowded around it, waving espresso cups and gesturing dramatically at imaginary trajectories in the dust.

Belinda and Noah sat down at the far end, their heads bent close together as they dissected something, probably Max's mid-match pitch invasion, while the dog himself lay blissfully sprawled at their feet, tongue lolling in sleepy contentment. Every few minutes, Belinda's laugh floated down the table, warm and unselfconscious, and each time Noah's head tipped just slightly toward her, as though drawn by instinct.

Carla noticed. Carla noticed everything. She'd found herself wedged between two old-timers, one of whom was Mikiel, who looked extremely pleased with himself. The fisherman had the weathered, permanently wind-kissed face of a man who had spent a lifetime out on the sea, and the mischievous grin of someone who had spent just as long meddling in other people's business. He elbowed Carla, nearly making her slosh her drink. Then he jerked his chin toward the far end of the table.

'Do you see what I see?' he murmured, voice heavy with glee.

Carla followed his gaze. Belinda was leaning in to say something to Noah, her shoulder brushing his. Noah was pretending not to notice that he'd practically melted into his chair. Carla smirked. 'I do indeed. Unfortunately, those two are apparently both blind and stupid.'

Mikiel slapped the table triumphantly. 'Exactly! The boy is like a fish who doesn't realise he's already in the net.'

'And Belinda,' Carla added dryly, 'is like a fish who thinks the net is just a fun little hammock.'

'Ha!' Mikiel barked, thoroughly delighted. 'Then we must bring them together. Give them… what do you call it… quality time.'

Carla leaned forward conspiratorially. 'Agreed. What are you thinking, Captain Cupid?'

Mikiel scratched his face thoughtfully, eyes twinkling. 'A day on the boat. Sun. Sea. Nowhere to escape each other.'

Carla nodded approvingly. 'And you know what makes that perfect? Belinda hates climbing onto boats. Noah will have to help her, and I will pretend to have sudden, tragic vertigo, or something that prevents me from going.

Mikiel wheezed a laugh. 'Excellent! And food. We make the boy cook. Good food always makes the heart softer.'

'And wine the inhibitions lower,' Carla added, waggling her eyebrows. 'I like the way your devious fisherman mind works, old man.'

A short while later, just as they were polishing off a shared bowl of olives, a curious shadow fell over them. 'What are you up to, old man?' Noah asked, amusement colouring his tone. 'Carla is far too young for you.' Mikiel sputtered indignantly as Carla preened.

'Don't be cheeky, boy! We were simply arranging a lovely outing for all of us tomorrow. On my boat. This young lady,' he thumped Carla's shoulder with surprising fondness, 'is desperate to see Manoel Island.'

Carla nodded enthusiastically, beaming. 'Absolutely desperate.'

'What, all of us?' Noah asked, eyebrow raised, gaze flicking briefly toward Belinda as she chatted with another of the old players.

'Yes!' Carla said brightly. 'And you can make us a lovely picnic. Very romantic. I mean, uh, rustic.' She coughed.

Noah blinked. 'I'm happy to make a picnic, sure. But I'm not sure…'

'No arguments,' Mikiel said, slapping the table in a way that made several espresso cups jump. 'Respect your elders and grant this ancient man his wishes.'

Noah stared at him, baffled. Mikiel never took days out for pleasure cruises. Ever. The man practically lived on his boat and still claimed he didn't have time for "frivolous nonsense." But he shrugged, slow and good-naturedly. 'Alright, alright. If you insist.'

He bent to scratch Max behind the ears, and the dog thumped his tail approvingly. Straightening, Noah added, 'I'd better take this troublemaker home before he starts another match. Mikiel, I'll see you tomorrow. Carla, Belle, see you both at dinner.'

He left with Max trotting happily beside him, and Mikiel leaned toward Carla, grinning like a man who had just secured the perfect catch. Carla lifted her glass. 'Operation Manoel Island is officially underway.' They clinked. And down the table, Belinda watched Noah leave with a soft expression she didn't even realise she was wearing.

Dinner that night was a relaxed affair, the three of them now comfortable with each other in a way that felt more like old friends than chef and guests. Noah had whipped up a simple pasta dish that tasted divine, followed by a lemon sorbet that was equally heavenly. Carla kept smirking to herself as she thought about the plan for tomorrow and started to lay the groundwork for her part in the charade. 'I think I'll call it a night, Belinda,' she said after refusing a top-up of wine. 'My head isn't feeling great.'

'Probably the after-effects of last night,' she replied, but looked at her with concern. 'Can I get you something? I have some painkillers upstairs.'

'No, it's alright. I have some. I'm sure a couple of tablets and a good night's sleep will stave off whatever this is.' She rose and gave her friend a kiss on the cheek before going up to her room. A huge smile broke out on her face as soon as her back was turned. Her skills at acting were certainly coming in useful this trip.

Hopefully, Operation Manoel Island would have the desired outcome.

Chapter Nineteen

When Carla hadn't appeared for breakfast by ten the next morning, Belinda finally abandoned her toast and padded upstairs. She hesitated only a moment before gently pushing open her friend's bedroom door. The room was kept in heavy morning darkness, shutters barely cracked, but a faint rustling under the duvet told her Carla was awake. 'Belinda, is that you?' came a croaky, pitiful little call.

'Yes, Carla, it's me,' Belinda said, stepping inside and closing the door quietly behind her. As her eyes adjusted, she could make out the dramatic sprawl of Carla half-covered in blankets, one leg poking out like some Renaissance painting of a saint in distress. 'What's going on? Breakfast service finished ages ago, and you're still lolling about up here. That's very unlike you.'

Carla groaned with Oscar-worthy commitment and draped the back of her hand over her forehead. 'I have… one of my heads,' she whispered, with the solemnity of a doomed queen. 'I can't possibly get up.'

'You mean a migraine?'

Carla nodded, then winced in theatrical agony. 'Terrible. Catastrophic. Utterly disabling.'

Belinda frowned. She had known Carla for so many years and had never once heard mention of migraines. But maybe… maybe stress? Heat? Wine tasting plus more wine plus the extra-special wine she'd bought from Zachary? 'Well, if that's the case, we'll just postpone the boat trip. It's fine.'

'No!' Carla blurted, then tried again in her frail, quivering voice. 'No, please don't. I would feel even worse if you didn't go because of me.'

Belinda blinked. That was unusually selfless for Carla at the best of times. 'It's no problem, really,' Belinda began, but Carla cut her off with surprising firmness.

'I insist,' she said, sounding suddenly robust for someone moments earlier on the brink of death. Then she added a moan and flopped sideways for effect. Belinda raised an eyebrow. Something was decidedly off, but the idea of a day on the water like old times with Noah and Mikiel tugged at her heart more than she cared to admit.

'If you're sure. Can I get you anything?'

'A cold compress, it sometimes it helps,' Carla murmured, turning her head away just in time to hide her self-satisfied smile. She coughed weakly for good measure.

Back downstairs, Noah was in the kitchen finishing the last of the breakfast cleanup and packing a picnic hamper that looked comically large for four people. Or rather, for three now. Belinda stepped in. 'Carla has a migraine. She's not going to make it today.'

Noah's face fell instantly. 'Oh. Should we rearrange? I can call Mikiel.'

'She insists we still go,' Belinda said, unable to keep the exasperation out of her voice. 'Does the villa have cold compresses?'

'Yes, of course.' Noah dug around in the freezer, producing one triumphantly. 'I'll tell Sofia not to come by today so she doesn't disturb her. Leave Carla her number too, just in case she needs anything.'

Belinda nodded, feeling guilty but not enough to completely quash the little flutter in her chest at the prospect of a day out that involved Noah. She took the compress upstairs, checked on Carla, who whispered thank you as though she were speaking on her deathbed, then finally went to get ready.

When they reached the port, however, the scene was pure drama. Mikiel was pacing along the pier like a storm-swollen heron, shouting into his phone in Maltese and gesticulating wildly. He ended the call with an impressive expletive and whirled around. 'Those *losers* from yesterday are contesting the result! As if your dog jumping around the pitch changed anything. Pah!'

'I'm sorry,' Noah muttered, grimacing.

'It's not your fault, boy. It's those idiots.' Mikiel waved dismissively. 'Now I have to go to a meeting to clear this all up! Uwejja, unbelievable.' His gaze darted around theatrically. 'Where is Carla?'

'She's not feeling well,' Belinda sighed. 'Looks like we're fated not to go today.'

'Don't be ridiculous.' Mikiel jabbed a finger at them. 'You two go. Noah knows exactly how to handle my boat, if memory serves. It would be criminal to waste such a beautiful day and all that food.' He pointed at the hamper Noah was carrying as if it contained the crown jewels.

Belinda exchanged a look with Noah, who shrugged helplessly but not unhappily.

'I guess we could,' she said cautiously.

'Of course you can!' Mikiel boomed. 'You've plenty of fuel, and I left a couple of bottles of my homemade wine in the fridge. Take them. Enjoy. Relax!' He clapped Noah on the back hard enough to make him stumble. Before either of them could protest, Mikiel was already marching off along the harbour front, phone in hand, muttering about "bloody amateurs" and "boċċi politics," but wearing a grin that stretched from ear to ear.

Belinda stared after him. Noah stared after him. Then they looked at each other.

'Well,' Belinda said faintly, 'I guess we're going.'

Noah's smile was small but unmistakably warm. 'Looks like it.'

And far up in the villa, behind shuttered windows, Carla lay in bed, holding her phone, having just received a text from Mikiel: *Success. They are alone. Operation Manoel Island is underway.* Carla grinned and tucked the covers around her like a cocoon of triumph.

Belinda accepted Noah's helping hand as she climbed onto the boat. A small thrill ran through her at his touch, but there was a frown on her face. 'I smell a rat,' she said as she sat on the banquette.

Noah looked about, confused. 'A rat? All I smell is fish and sea, and Mikiel takes good care of his boat.'

She laughed. 'No, I mean, don't you find it at all suspicious that both Carla and Mikiel are unable to make it today?' She arched an eyebrow at him, waiting for the penny to drop. A slow smile crossed his face as it dawned on him, and he started to chuckle.

'Good grief, crafty old bugger,' he said, shaking his head in amusement. 'I was really worried Max had ruined the game.' He looked concerned for a moment. 'Are you sure you still want to go?'

Belinda didn't hesitate. 'Yes, of course. After all, what harm can it do?'

Chapter Twenty

Noah wasn't surprised when Belinda let out a belly laugh a short while later, looked at him, and said, 'they have completely set us up, haven't they?'

He let out a soft huff of laughter. 'Oh, absolutely. We're victims of a coordinated ambush.'

'My so-called friend Carla faked it, didn't she?'

'About as convincingly as Max fakes limping when he wants extra treats.'

Belinda laughed, shaking her head, 'and Mikiel?'

'Has the subtlety of a foghorn.' Noah lifted the hamper onto the boat. 'He's probably halfway through bragging to someone already.'

Onboard the familiar creak of the wooden deck settled something deep in Noah's chest. Being back on the water always did. He busied himself with ropes and switches, partly because he needed to, partly because it was easier than looking at Belle too long and remembering how she had laughed at dinner the night before, head thrown back, catching the candlelight like she was made of sunshine.

She perched on the bench seat, sunglasses pushed into her hair. 'Ready when you are, Captain.' Captain. She didn't mean anything by it, but the words hit him square in the ribs. He cleared his throat.

'Alright then.'

They pushed off, and soon the small fishing boat was cutting gently through the blue-green water, the hum of the engine blending with the cry of distant gulls. Belinda leaned on the railing, hair whipping in the wind, looking out toward the pale outline of Manoel Island. Sunlight danced on the water, turning everything gold around her. He should've kept his eyes on the horizon. He didn't.

'So,' she said after a while. 'Carla pretends to die of a headache. Mikiel gets mysteriously summoned by the boċċi elders. And somehow, we end up alone on a boat together.'

'Tragic coincidence,' Noah said.

She bumped her shoulder lightly against his. 'Mm-hmm. They're lucky I like you.'

His heart stalled, then thudded again. 'Oh? You like me?'

She turned, smiling slightly. 'I always did. That's the problem.'

He swallowed. Hard. Thankfully, Manoel Island grew larger on the horizon, and he focused on navigating toward a hidden cove he hadn't visited in years, a small, pale crescent of sand tucked between rocks, reachable only by boat. When they drifted near, Belinda gasped softly.

'It's beautiful,' she whispered. The world felt suddenly quiet. Just them, the sea and the sun. He dropped anchor and rubbed the back of his neck.

'Want to swim?'

'I didn't come just to sightsee,' she said, already untying her cover-up. 'So yes.'

He snorted, averting his eyes, but not before the image of her in a bright red bikini was imprinted on his brain. Noah fastened the ladder and followed her into the cool, turquoise water. She let out a squeal as she hit the surface, then disappeared beneath it in a shimmer of bubbles. When she came back up, slick hair pushed back, cheeks flushed with laughter, he forgot how to breathe. Belle splashed him. He retaliated. Soon he was chasing her lazily in the shallows, their laughter echoing off the limestone cliffs. It felt easy. Natural. Like something he'd forgotten he loved.

After a while they climbed back on board, sun-warmed and breathless, and he unpacked the picnic: roasted vegetable tarts, marinated olives, fresh bread from the bakery, and the prawns he'd grilled early that morning. Her smile when she saw it made every minute worth it.

'You've outdone yourself,' she said softly as she bit into a tart.

He poured the homemade wine, rose-gold, crisp, smelling faintly of peaches and sea air. They drank, chatting about old adventures, legs stretched out, toes brushing accidentally, now-and-then-on-purpose. 'This is perfect,' she murmured, watching the sunlight scatter on the water.

'It could be worse,' he teased lightly, even as his chest tightened.

She looked at him then. Really looked. 'Noah, I'm really glad I came back.'

The breeze shifted. The boat rocked gently. And Noah realised this was the first time in five years that a moment had felt like the start of something instead of the shadow of something lost. For a moment the air felt different, thicker, warmer, shimmering faintly with something more dangerous than the homemade wine.

Noah's breath hitched almost imperceptibly. 'Belle…'

She swallowed. 'Hmm?'

He hesitated, and she saw the exact moment a sliver of fear crossed his face. The old hurt. The carefulness he wrapped around himself like armour. But then she shifted slightly closer, just enough for their knees to touch fully, and the fear flickered, then softened. 'I'm glad you're here,' he said. It wasn't dramatic or rehearsed. Just quietly honest. 'More than I expected to be.'

Her heart fluttered, wild and painful and sweet all at once. 'I'm glad too.' Silence settled over the boat, calm, expectant, stretching taut between them. The boat rocked gently. A gull cried overhead. Somewhere below, the anchor chain clicked rhythmically against the hull.

Belinda reached out first. Just a brush of her fingers against the back of his hand. Barely anything. But Noah inhaled sharply, as if he'd been waiting for that exact touch and fearing it at the same time. He turned his hand beneath hers slowly, giving her time to pull away. She didn't. Instead, she let her fingers slip into his. Warm and certain. He lifted his gaze to hers, dark, searching, hopeful. She felt her breath catch, her chest tighten, her entire body go still.

And then Noah leaned in. Not all the way. Just far enough that she could feel the ghost of his breath on her lips, warm and uncertain.

'Belle, if I'm misreading this…?'

'You're not,' she whispered.

That was all he needed. His hand came up to her cheek, tentative, thumb brushing lightly across her skin as if relearning the map of her face. She leaned into his touch, heart thudding so hard she wondered if the entire island could hear it. And then finally he closed the last inch. The kiss was soft at first. Testing, searching, a gentle question. She answered with equal gentleness, her lips moving against his in a slow, warm tug that felt like rediscovering something once lost. His fingers slid into her damp hair. She curled a hand against his jaw. The world around them dissolved into sun and salt and the faint taste of homemade wine on his mouth. When they finally pulled apart, both breathless, the moment held them suspended, half-laughing, half stunned.

'Wow,' she murmured.

Noah huffed a soft laugh, forehead resting against hers. 'Yeah. Wow.'

And in the quiet glow of the Maltese afternoon, with the boat rocking gently beneath them and the taste of the sea still clinging to their skin, Noah realised something he hadn't felt in a very long time, hope didn't hurt anymore.

Chapter Twenty-One

Belinda's heart was racing; she couldn't ever remember a kiss from her husband lighting up her insides this way. As if every nerve ending was a firework waiting to go off. The thought of Mike made her pull back. God, what was she doing? Barely divorced and kissing someone on a boat in Malta! Maybe this was the famous midlife crisis she'd heard so much about. 'We should get back,' she said abruptly, standing and pulling her coverup tightly around her.

Noah looked like he'd been slapped, but just nodded and said, 'Okay, then.' She started to clear away the remains of the picnic while he busied himself with pulling up the anchor and getting ready to set sail. She placed a hand on his arm.

'I don't regularly go around kissing people, just so you know. It's just…'

'You still have feelings for your husband?'

'Ex-husband, and no. Not nice ones anyway.' She stared out at the water for a moment. 'It's just, I don't know. Being here has brought up a lot of memories, and a lot of feelings.

We were always such good friends. I'd hate for anything to spoil that.'

Noah looked thoughtful for a second, then leaned forward until she could feel his breath on her cheek. 'How about we stay good friends? Just good friends who kiss occasionally?' Then he closed the gap and brushed his lips, almost imperceptibly, against hers. When he pulled away, her eyes were dark with desire, but she giggled.

'You always did know how to improve things.'

Back at the harbour, they stood awkwardly. Out at sea, away from real life, it had been easy, but both were unsure how to be with each other now. Noah coughed.

'We didn't discuss whether you need dinner.'

'No, it's fine. Technically you made lunch,' she smiled. 'So, we'll see you in the morning, if Carla has recovered, of course.'

He grinned at that but said, 'Ah, tomorrow is my day off. But the housekeeper will be there to put on the coffee and lay out some pastries for you.'

Belinda frowned for a beat. 'We haven't seen a housekeeper. I hadn't even thought about how the place was always clean and our beds were made up.'

'That's because we try to arrange for her to come while you're out, the magic of Sublime Retreats!' he said with flamboyant jazz hands. 'Although I forgot to tell her Carla was there today, I hope she didn't disturb her.'

Back at the villa, she found Carla lounging happily by the pool, a glass of wine in one hand and a book in the other. 'I take it you're feeling better?' She said, unable to keep the scorn out of her voice.

'Oh, yes. That cold compress worked a treat,' she replied with a demure smile. 'How was your day?'

'It was… nice,' Belinda replied, flopping onto the sunbed next to Carla's.

'Nice? Just nice?' she demanded, sounding affronted.

Belinda smiled to herself. 'Yes, I think that's a good word for it.'

Carla huffed and puffed for a while before suddenly sitting up and asking, 'how old is this place?'

'I'm not sure exactly, a couple of hundred years, I think. Why?'

'I think it's haunted,' she whispered, looking around with gigantic eyes. 'I heard some noises earlier, but whenever I looked there was no one there. But I kept catching a glimpse of a shadowy figure from the corner of my eye.'

Realising immediately that the housekeeper had been, and obviously tried to stay out of the way of the guest, Belinda felt a moment of impishness. Time for a little payback, she thought to herself. 'Wow, the company mentioned there had been sightings of a woman, but I didn't take it seriously.'

Carla paled slightly; she took such things very seriously, as Belinda well knew. 'Do you think the ghost wanted something from me?' she asked in a tremulous voice.

'Oh, I doubt that,' she replied blithely. 'Apparently it only appears when there are devious people here. You know, liars, double-crossers, people who like to hoodwink others,' she added for good measure, looking away to hide her grin.

Carla choked a little before saying in a small voice, 'I guess I'm okay then.'

Belinda arranged her expression into something saintly and innocent. 'Oh yes, of course you are,' she said, patting Carla's arm with mock sympathy.

Carla narrowed her eyes. 'You're enjoying this.'

'Me? Never. I've been traumatised all day by the thought of you alone here with… mysterious shadows.'

Carla took a large steadying gulp of wine. 'Well, I'm glad you're back now. Safety is in numbers.'

Belinda snorted. 'Don't worry. If the ghost comes for you, I'll shout helpful advice from behind the sofa.'

'You're a terrible friend,' Carla grumbled, but she leaned over and bumped their shoulders together. They sat in companionable silence for a few moments, the pool shimmering turquoise in the fading light, the villa humming with the soft, ancient quiet of thick stone walls. Belinda let her head fall back against the sunbed, feeling the pleasant ache in her limbs from swimming and, well, other activities that had nothing to do with swimming.

Carla waited, because of course she did, before turning slightly and asking in her most casual voice. 'Sooo. Nothing interesting happened today?'

Belinda made a small, strangled sound. 'Nope. Totally ordinary. Although strangely, Mikiel couldn't make it either.' She gave her friend a sideways glance, but she gave nothing away.

'Right.' Carla nodded sagely. 'You spent the day on a boat with a tall, handsome, extremely single man who looks at you like you hung the moon and nothing remotely noteworthy occurred.' Belinda was suddenly fascinated by her toenails. Carla gasped loudly. 'OH MY GOD, YOU KISSED HIM.'

Belinda slapped a hand over her mouth. 'Shhh! The ghost will hear you!'

'I knew it!' Carla swatted her arm. 'I saw the way he looked at you at the match. Like he was about to propose or burst into flames. Possibly both.'

Belinda covered her face with both hands. 'It was just a little kiss.'

'Was it, though?' Carla waggled her eyebrows. 'Was it a sweet, gentle, demure brief peck? Or was it,' she made a dramatic swooning motion, 'a heart-thumping, toe-curling, midlife-crisis-inducing lip-lock of destiny?'

She peeked through her fingers. 'Well, my toes curled a little.' Carla shrieked into her wineglass. 'Stop! It's not. It's complicated,' Belinda insisted, sitting up. 'I panicked. Mike popped into my head, and I had this whole moment of, of guilt, I guess? Or confusion? Or something equally annoying.'

Carla softened immediately. 'Honey, that's normal. You're freshly divorced. Your heart's doing a sort of emotional defragging.'

Belinda blinked. 'A what?'

'You know. All the files are being reorganised. Some trash is being deleted. New updates are installing.' Carla tapped her temple. 'It's a whole thing.'

Belinda laughed despite herself. Carla set her wine down and took Belinda's hand.

'But seriously, did the kiss make you feel good? Not guilty. Not confused. Just… good?'

Letting out a slow breath, the memory washed warm through her. 'Yes. Extremely good.'

Carla beamed. 'Then that's your answer.'

Belinda hesitated, a smile tugging at her lips. 'He suggested we stay good friends who kiss occasionally.'

Carla's mouth fell open. 'Oh my God, he's perfect. Do you know what I would give for a friend like that?'

'You'd be uncontrollable.'

'Exactly! So grab him before I do.'

They both dissolved into laughter, leaning into each

other, the sky turning rosy above them. The villa's external lights flickered on, warm and golden, and Belinda felt a flutter of nerves, of excitement, of possibility. Carla squeezed her hand. 'Seriously, Belinda. You deserve something good. Something easy. Something that makes your insides light up like the Millennium Fireworks.'

Her heart gave a small, traitorous hop. Maybe, just maybe, she could let herself have that. Carla raised her wineglass. 'To ghosts, kisses, and conveniently handsome Maltese men.'

Belinda clinked her glass with a laugh. 'And to friends who scheme relentlessly.'

Her friend grinned at her. 'You're welcome.'

Chapter Twenty-Two

When Noah woke up the next morning, he found himself grinning before he even got out of bed. It was ridiculous, really. He was forty-six years old, not some excitable teenager waking up after his first school disco. But there it was, that stupid, unstoppable grin stretching across his face. Max, sensing his excitement like only a dog could, launched himself into a triumphant lap of the bedroom, nails clicking against the tiles, tail wagging so furiously it could've powered a small generator. He yapped at Noah's ankles all the way to the kitchen.

'Okay, okay,' Noah laughed, leaning down to rub behind Max's ears until the dog melted bonelessly against his leg. 'Breakfast first.'

He reached up to the top shelf, the sacred place where he kept the dog food safe from Max's ingenious attempts at burglary. Just last week, Max had managed to nose open the pantry door, topple a box of cereal, and attempt to chew through the rice bag. If he'd had opposable thumbs, he'd probably be running a small supermarket by now.

He'd had plans for his day off. Good, solid, productive plans. The kind that makes you feel like a responsible adult who deserves a gold star. First on the list, finally painting the lounge. After that, he'd head to the dog shelter for his late afternoon shift, cleaning the runs, feeding the dogs, letting them crawl all over him for affection. But now? The thought of going an entire day without seeing Belle made something in his chest twist unpleasantly. Or pleasantly. He wasn't sure yet.

Maybe I could message her, he thought as he made his coffee. He had Sophia's contact sheet, guest numbers neatly printed, stuffed in his bag. Just in case he ever needed to call someone about a change in menu or plans. Max inhaled his food at alarming speed, then nudged Noah's calf with insistent determination. Noah grabbed his coffee and his bag, opened the back door onto the sun-washed terrace, and stepped outside into the soft breeze scented with rosemary and sea salt. Max sprinted off into the scrubby garden, probably hunting for nonexistent rabbits. He'd never caught one in his life, but hope sprang eternal.

Noah sat at the little wrought-iron table, staring out at the sparkling water below. What could he even say to her? "Good morning, thanks again for the kiss, how's the weather?" He winced. Smooth as sandpaper. It had been a long, long time since he'd felt this nervous about contacting a woman. His stomach did a strange, swooping thing that he pretended was the coffee being too strong. He pulled out his phone, thumbs hovering. He typed the first digit of her number and froze.

What was he doing? The grin slid off his face.

Yesterday had been… unexpected. Wonderful, yes, but also complicated. He'd kissed Belle like a man starved of affection, and for a moment he'd allowed himself to imagine future things, dangerous things, without thinking. Not long ago, he'd been ready to spend his entire life with Sarah. Belle was part of his past, wasn't she? A bright, warm, reckless piece of his youth. Not someone he was meant to trip over again in middle age with a rescue dog and a house that still needed fixing.

The devil on his shoulder whispered that it was harmless. Belle was on holiday. This didn't have to be a big deal. The angel on the other side swatted that idea clean across the terrace. If he treated Belle like a bit of fleeting fun, what would that make him? And what would it say about what Sarah had meant to him? The arguments spun in fast circles until he felt dizzy. With a sharp exhale, he shoved the phone away and stood.

Painting. Yes. Painting would clear his head. Except it didn't. At all.

As he steadily coated the ancient limestone walls in soft, buttery yellow, a colour he'd chosen specifically to reflect the sunlight and warm up the cool stone, his brain kept jumping tracks. With one stroke, he was telling himself to be sensible. With the next, he was remembering how her laughter sounded across the water. Then he'd picture Sarah smiling, telling him to stop being an idiot. Then he'd picture Belle smiling back at him on the boat, soft and shy and full of possibilities.

He briefly considered walking down to the café to ask Mikiel for advice but instantly shook that off. He already knew the old man's stance; he'd said it many times, at many tables, after many glasses of wine. Sarah would want you to live. Not just exist. By the time the walls gleamed with their new colour and the room smelled pleasantly of fresh paint, Noah was no closer to clarity. But the clock was ticking toward his shelter shift, and his chest felt full, too full for him to ignore the one thing he knew he needed to do.

The cemetery was quiet when he arrived, the midday heat tempered by tall cypress trees that whispered in the wind. He crouched down in front of the headstone and gently cleared away the fallen petals and dried leaves. Then he placed a bunch of fresh roses, deep red, her favourite, in the vase.

'Hi, Sar,' he said softly. 'It's me.' He sat back on his heels. Talking to her still came naturally, even now. 'Sorry I haven't been in a while. Things have been a bit hectic.' He rubbed the back of his neck, searching for the right words. None felt quite right. 'The thing is, I've met someone.' He let out a short laugh. 'Or re-met, I suppose.' The breeze rustled the branches like a gentle nudge. 'She's… nice. Really nice. I think you'd like her.'

He paused, considering that. They would have liked each other. Belle's humour, Sarah's impish fun, they would've teamed up and teased him mercilessly. 'I'm not sure where this is going,' he admitted. 'Or if it's going anywhere at all. But I needed to tell you.' His voice went quiet. 'I still love you. You know that. I always will. But Belle,' He swallowed, eyes burning. 'Belle makes me feel alive again. Like there's still a future for me. One that isn't just this quiet, lonely routine.'

A butterfly drifted past and landed delicately on the stone. Noah let out a shaky breath. 'I don't know what to do. But I'm trying. I hope that's okay with you.'

He touched the edge of the headstone, then stood slowly, the weight in his chest a little lighter. Tomorrow, he decided, he would talk to Belle tomorrow.

Whatever happened next, he'd face it honestly.

Chapter Twenty-Three

Belinda woke earlier than expected, much earlier than a woman who'd had her entire emotional world rearranged on a boat should reasonably wake. But sunlight had a way of prying her eyelids apart, and the Maltese sun was basically a cosmic burglar with no respect for privacy or personal boundaries. She threw on a robe and padded to the kitchen terrace, expecting quiet. What she found instead was Carla standing frozen in the doorway like she'd seen a demon or, more accurately, like she'd seen one yesterday.

'Good morning,' said a small, stocky, silver-haired woman with a bun so tight it looked professionally engineered. She was laying out pastries, fruit, and still-warm ftira as if performing a sacred ceremony. Carla jumped a full foot in the air, clutching her chest. 'You!'

Magda blinked at her mildly. 'Me?' she asked, as if she was regularly greeted strangers with startled shrieks. Belinda bit the inside of her cheek. Hard.

Carla turned slowly to Belle, eyes wide with betrayal. 'That's her. The ghost. The ghost who haunted me.'

Magda, whose entire presence radiated no-nonsense Mediterranean aunt energy, stared at her. 'I am not a ghost,' she said dryly, 'but sometimes I wish I were, because then I could walk through walls instead of lugging linen baskets up and down your stairs.'

Belinda lost the battle not to laugh. Carla glared at her. 'You knew.' She lifted her mug innocently.

'Hmm? Who? Me? Never.'

Carla huffed, stomped to her chair, and proceeded to butter a croissant with the silent fury of a woman deeply wronged. Belinda sat, but her cheerful façade evaporated when her gaze snagged on the Sublime Retreats menu card propped on the table. The one with staff contacts on the back. The one with Noah's number neatly printed under "On-Site Chef."

Her traitorous heart gave a swoop. Her logical brain smacked it with a rolled-up newspaper. It's too soon; she'd barely survived the divorce. Mike had lied. About finances. About trips. About the woman from work who was "just a friend." She'd been blindsided so thoroughly she still flinched when her phone buzzed unexpectedly. And yet, there was Noah.

Sweet, solid, quietly warm Noah. She felt safe with him in a way she hadn't expected. But her life was in America. Her friends, her routine, her… well. Her Arhaus furniture. What was left for her in Boston? A house she'd chosen to raise a family, a new emptiness where a marriage used to be. Maybe she was having that midlife crisis. Maybe she should buy a sports car. Or take up pottery. Or stop kissing men on boats.

Before her brain could spiral further, she decided to get out. Clear her mind. Pay her respects. Her grandparents were buried at the little cemetery on the hill, the one with the terracotta pots and lazy cats sunbathing between graves.

'Going for a walk,' she told Carla.

'Enjoy,' Carla sniffed, still pretending she hadn't tried to exorcise a housekeeper yesterday.

Belinda strolled through Valletta's narrow streets, trying not to dissect every memory of Noah's mouth on hers. By the time she reached the cemetery gates, she almost felt calm. Nearly. She passed through the rows, pausing now and then to brush dust from familiar names. Her grandparents. The neighbours who used to sneak her lemon ices as a kid. It all felt grounding.

Then she heard a voice, soft, warm, male. Noah. She turned the corner and froze. He was standing in front of a grave, head bowed, new roses in the vase. Talking gently, affectionately, to the person beneath the stone. She opened her mouth to call out, but the way he spoke stopped her. The tenderness in it, the grief, the love. Stepping back into the shade, she raised her hand to her mouth. After another moment, he touched the headstone, whispered something she couldn't hear, and walked away with Max trotting faithfully at his heels.

Belinda waited until he was gone before she approached. Then she saw the name, Sarah Vella. His fiancée. The fiancée he'd lost on their wedding day. The fiancée he still brought roses to. A lump rose so sharply in her throat she practically swallowed her own heart.

'Oh,' she whispered, her vision misting. Of course. She pressed a hand over her face. Well, that was that. She'd kissed a man who was still very much in love with someone else. She let out a shaky, slightly hysterical laugh. 'Perfect, Belinda. Just perfect. You finally kiss someone new after decades, and he's emotionally taken. By a dead woman.

Great job.' She wiped her eyes, squared her shoulders, and whispered to Sarah's stone, 'honestly? You could've warned a girl.'

Then she turned and left the cemetery, determined never, ever to kiss Noah again. Probably.

Back at the villa, Belinda marched across the terrace like a woman with a mission, specifically, the mission of avoiding all feelings and possibly all men. She dropped her bag by her sunbed with a thud that startled a sunbathing gecko into sprinting for cover. Carla looked up from the pool, sunglasses perched halfway down her nose.

'Well, hello to you too, Thundercloud.'

'I am fine,' Belinda declared, which of course meant she was absolutely not fine.

Carla floated on her back, doing lazy starfish impressions. 'You know, when people say they're fine like that, what they really mean is, I just made a terrible life decision and now I'm spiraling.'

She huffed and unfolded her towel with unnecessary aggression. 'I did not make a terrible life decision.'

'Mm-hmm.' Carla paddled to the side and leaned her elbows on the pool edge. 'Then why are you acting like you just got dumped by a man who wasn't actually your boyfriend?'

Belinda froze mid-towel-fluff. 'I'm not.'

'You are.'

'I'm not.'

'You are. Honey, you look like someone stole your chocolate stash and replaced it with kale.'

Belinda cracked, groaning dramatically as she flopped onto her sunbed. 'I saw Noah at the cemetery.'

'O-kay…' Carla said slowly. 'Were you spying?'

'No!'

'Accidentally spying?'

She hesitated. 'I just happened to be cemetery-adjacent.'

Her friend smirked. 'Go on.'

'He was visiting Sarah's grave,' Belle whispered. 'Talking to her, bringing roses. Being… sweet. Heartbreaking. Loyal.'

Carla blinked. 'And this is a problem?'

Belinda stared up at the sky, squinting as if the sun itself had betrayed her. 'Because he still loves her, Carla. Deeply. Beautifully. Completely.' She sighed. 'Which is wonderful for him. Really. But it means I can't, we can't.'

'Oh my god,' Carla deadpanned, 'you think you're the rebound.'

She sat up indignantly. 'What?!'

'The woman men date after epic heartbreak but before they rejoin humanity. Like emotional training wheels.'

Belinda pressed a hand to her chest, affronted. 'I am nobody's training wheels.'

Carla hoisted herself out of the pool, dripping dramatically onto her sunbed so she couldn't escape. 'Belinda, listen to me.' She poked her shoulder. 'He kissed you. You kissed him. It was, based on your description, a very I-want-your-face sort of kiss.'

She went pink. 'That's not, well, Carla!'

Carla smirked. 'And the man has eyes for you. Real eyes. Not casual-friendly-hot chef eyes.'

'But he was talking to his dead fiancée's grave an hour ago!'

'Yes,' she said slowly, 'because he loved her. And he misses her. And he's a decent human with feelings. Grief doesn't flip off like a light switch. But it doesn't mean he can't care about someone new.'

Belinda stared at her, uncertain, and she softened. 'What did he say to you on the boat?'

She mumbled, 'that we could be good friends. Friends who kiss occasionally.'

Carla cackled. 'Exactly! That's practically a marriage proposal in guy language; that's basically him building you a house.'

Belinda snorted despite herself. 'It is not.'

'Sweetheart.' Carla sat beside her, touching her hand gently. 'You deserve joy, and connection, and someone who makes your toes curl. The fact he's a good man who loved someone before you? That's not a red flag. That's a green one; are you that emotionally colorblind that you can't see that?'

She sagged, torn. 'But my life is in Boston.'

Carla arched her brow. 'Is it, though?'

She hesitated, and Carla gave her a meaningful look. Belinda flopped back. 'It doesn't matter, anyway. I am not getting together with the hot chef.'

Carla smirked. 'Uh-huh, sure. I'll just tell the universe you're passing on that opportunity. I'm sure someone else will snap him up.'

She shot upright. 'Who?! What someone?!'

Carla grinned wickedly. 'Ah yes. Totally not interested.'

Belinda groaned into her hands as Carla cackled and reached for the wine.

Chapter Twenty-Four

Noah had received a text from Sophia overnight that there would be another couple arriving at the villa this afternoon. It must be the son arriving, he thought, then wondered why Belle hadn't messaged herself. His contact details were there in plain sight after all. Maybe she was embarrassed after… Well after everything that had happened on the boat.

The routine of preparing breakfast service didn't calm him the way it usually did. He was jumpy. That damn gecko was staring at him again, from the shelf next to the cooker this time, and every creak made him fizz with anticipation, thinking it might be her. It was actually Carla who appeared first, taking her place serenely at the table, but the wicked grin on her face told him she knew everything.

'So,' she said casually, reaching for a pastry. 'I gather you guys had fun on the boat?'

'I gather your migraine disappeared as soon as we set sail,' he batted back with a scowl.

Carla froze mid-bite, then raised her pastry at him in

salute, touché. Belinda walked out at that moment and took in the scene. 'What's going on?' she demanded of Carla.

'We were just talking about how much you enjoyed the boat ride.'

'Stop it,' Belinda hissed, taking her seat.

'Stop what?' she asked innocently. They glared at each other, the silent communication of two women who had been friends long enough to telepathically exchange threats.

'Sophia tells me we have more people arriving today.' Desperate to prevent bloodshed, or worse, another round of boat interrogation, Noah stepped in. 'You know, you could have just messaged me directly. My details are right there,' he nodded to the menu, where his number did, in fact, sit openly, proudly, helpfully.

'Yes, Belinda. Why didn't you just message him directly?' Carla sing-songed, receiving a kick under the table for her efforts.

'I didn't want to disturb you,' she mumbled, grabbing her coffee mug for something to do, but it was empty. With a smile, Noah picked up the coffee jug and poured it for her. 'Thank you,' she mumbled again, eyes fixed on the steam rising from the mug.

'So, dinner tonight?' he asked brightly. 'Any ideas on what you want, any allergies or anything I should know about?'

'No, no. Nothing like that; they're pretty easygoing.'

Carla snorted, 'I wouldn't call Alicia easy going, she's pretty high-maintenance if you ask me.'

'I'm sure she'll be fine,' Belinda chirped, ignoring Carla. 'Noah, just prepare what you like, your favourite meal perhaps?'

'Sure,' he said. 'I'll make something special for you.'

A silence followed that statement. Belinda drank her

coffee with exaggerated calm; Noah adjusted a napkin that didn't need adjusting before awkwardly making excuses and going back inside. Carla sat back, arms folded with a smile, enjoying the emotional chaos like it was a binge-worthy Netflix show.

That afternoon, as she was waiting with growing excitement for her son's arrival, Belinda received a call from her daughter. 'Annalise, honey! How are you?'

'I'm fine, Mom, sorry it's taken so long to get back to you.'

'That's okay, I just assumed you were busy creating something marvelous,' she smiled into the phone.

'Er, yes. I have been busy. Have you spoken to Dad recently?'

'Your father and I don't have that much cause to speak these days, honey,' Belinda replied, wondering what had brought this on.

'Maybe you should, you know, talk to him. I don't think he's happy, Mom.'

She bit back the reply that was on the tip of her tongue, one that involved people making beds and then lying in them, and instead just murmured, 'Oh, I'm sure he'll be fine.' Annalise had always been a daddy's girl, and the last few months had been tough for her too.

'Listen, I'm coming to Malta. My flight gets in tomorrow.'

'Oh my, that's wonderful news,' Belinda exclaimed. And it was. She couldn't remember the last time she'd had both her kids with her. 'Jason arrives today, so we'll have a full house.'

There was a slight pause. 'I was planning to bring someone with me if that's okay?'

'Sure, why not? The more, the merrier. I guess this someone is significant if you're bringing him with you?'

Annalise giggled. 'I think he might be Mom. I think he's *the one.*'

Slightly surprised, as her wild and carefree daughter had never shown any interest in settling down, Belinda said mildly, 'then I look forward to meeting him. Send me the flight details, and I'll get the driver to pick you up.'

When she closed the call, Carla was looking at her expectantly. 'I gather my goddaughter is joining us?'

'Yes, and she's bringing a significant other with her!'

'Interesting. At least they'll both be here for your birthday.'

'God, I'd forgotten about that,' Belinda laughed because it was true. With everything that had been going on, it had completely slipped her mind.

'You're just in denial. Don't worry; turning fifty is not the end of the world. And now you have an excuse to message the hot chef directly. That's if you're not too scared.'

'What? Why would I be scared?' She retorted, although she absolutely was.

'Oh, I don't know. Opening communications with someone you have feelings for can be pretty daunting,' her friend replied with a knowing grin.

'It's not, I'm not… For goodness' sake, Carla. I've decided to forget about all that nonsense; it's too complicated. I just want to concentrate on spending time with the kids and enjoying my time here.'

'Uh huh, sure you have. Well, if the hot-chef is now just the chef, no reason you can't message him and tell him about new guests arriving, is there?'

Belinda's heart gave a judder at the thought, but

wanting to prove Carla wrong forced her to stand and say bravely, 'In fact, I'll do it right now.'

A staccato of beeps outside announced the arrival of the driver with her son, saved by the horn, she thought, and rushed to the front door. And there he was, her tall, beautiful boy, looking as smart as ever in chinos and a button-down blue shirt that brought out his eyes. She wrapped him in a hug before stepping back and looking around him.

'Where's Alicia?'

The bright smile that had been on Jason's face fell. 'Alicia and I split up, Mom.'

'Oh, honey. What happened?'

'Let the boy in and give him a drink before you start grilling him,' said Carla, shoving her out of the way to reach up and give him a peck on the cheek. 'Handsome as ever, Jason. Come on in.'

As they trooped down the hall, Carla looked back at her. 'You better message *the* chef and let him know there's only one extra for dinner; we wouldn't want him going overboard preparing food, would we?'

Chapter Twenty-Five

Noah was at home, shifting a small coffee table back into place in his newly painted lounge when his phone buzzed. The number lighting up the screen was unfamiliar… but the country code was American. And there was only one American in his life causing his stomach to flip like a pancake at brunch. Belle. He wiped suddenly clammy palms on his shorts and opened the message.

Hi Noah, it's just one extra for dinner tonight. Long story. But there will be another two more arriving tomorrow.

Plain, efficient. Nothing flirty. No hint of, "I can't stop thinking about the kisses and your ridiculous smile." He reread it four times. Then five. Searching, like a code breaker during a war, for any sign that she was smiling when she typed. Nothing. The message was as emotionally revealing as a tax form. Still, she'd texted. He leaned against the wall and tapped out a reply:

Thanks for letting me know, Belle. I look forward to hearing the long story. Maybe over a coffee or a glass of wine?

He stared at it. Too much? Too little? Not enough

emojis? Should he add a winking face? No, absolutely not. He was a grown man. A professional. A chef. He would not communicate like a man who lived off Wi-Fi and chaos. 'What do you think, Max?' he asked the dog. Max barked enthusiastically, tail wagging so hard his whole body wiggled. 'You'd jump off a cliff if I asked, mate. Not helpful.' Still, encouragement was encouragement. Before he could lose his nerve, Noah hit send. Then immediately regretted being a bold, reckless fool with a complete lack of self-preservation.

Back at the villa, Belinda saw the message pop up. Her heart did a weird backflip, like a child who'd just discovered a new skipping rope and fairy wings. He wanted coffee or wine. Or both. With her. Pressing a hand to her chest, she smiled, and then resolutely put the phone face-down on the table. She did not have the bandwidth for swooning right now. She was mid-conversation with her son, who looked like a kicked puppy.

'So let me get this straight,' she said slowly. 'You've been trying for a baby for over a year, but Alicia was still on the pill?'

Jason nodded miserably. 'Yup.'

Carla gasped so hard she nearly swallowed her sunglasses. 'Bitch,' she declared in a stage whisper.

'Carla, please,' Belle murmured, though honestly, she agreed.

'Apparently, she doesn't want kids, Mom,' Jason continued. 'She likes our life the way it is, clean apartment, spontaneous weekends away, brunches with friends. She admitted it only when I suggested getting checked. Like maybe it was me.'

Belle's heart cracked clean in half. 'Honey…'

He shrugged, defeated. 'I guess she didn't know what she wanted until she really thought about it.'

Carla made a disgusted sound that could peel paint. 'So instead of talking, she doubled down on prenatal vitamins for you and took birth control for her?'

'That's not inaccurate,' Jason sighed.

Belinda squeezed his arm. 'Maybe space is exactly what you both need, to figure out what you truly want. And selfishly, I'm thrilled to have you here. Even under these circumstances.' She brightened. 'And good news, your sister arrives tomorrow!'

'With a significant someone,' Carla chimed in, wiggling eyebrows like she was auditioning for a cartoon villain.

Jason groaned. 'Oh great. Probably another flaky artist who wants to "cleanse my chakras" like the last one.'

Carla gasped. 'In fairness, that man had a very calming presence.'

'He tried to burn sage in my sock drawer.'

'Well, he thought your feet were haunted,' Carla said solemnly, but with a sly grin on her face.

Belinda laughed despite herself. Then the laughter faded as Noah returned to her thoughts, his lips soft and sure, his eyes full of warmth she hardly trusted. Lovely Noah, confusing Noah, waiting-for-a-reply-Noah. What should she do? Part of her was desperate to spend some more time alone with him; another part thought that it was a ridiculous idea. She was just here on holiday, and summer flings were not her style. Belinda knew if she got emotionally invested, it would just be too painful when she left, and she'd had enough heartbreak to last a lifetime.

No, thank you.

Seeing Jason and Carla staring at her expectantly, she straightened. 'This was probably the best idea you've had in ages, Carla,' she said brightly. 'A boat trip for my birthday, with both kids. And hopefully, no migraines this time.' Carla beamed with zero shame.

Noah was 100% not beaming. He refreshed his messages again. Seen, but no response. Brilliant, fantastic, spectacularly awkward. He was going to have to cook dinner for her, with the memory of that kiss slapping him every time she reached for a fork. He'd planned Stuffat tal-fenek, his grandmother's rabbit stew, comforting, delicious, and requiring hours of simmering over low heat in the villa kitchen. Which meant hours in her presence. With Belle, possibly ignoring him. And probably looking radiant while doing it.

Max nudged his leg sympathetically. 'Yeah, yeah. I know,' Noah groaned. 'I've made a stew of my entire life.' Max yipped. Noah flopped onto the couch, stared at the ceiling, and wished, just briefly, that he'd never learned to cook. Never kissed a beautiful American woman on a sun-drenched Maltese boat, and never fallen headfirst into the kind of trouble that tasted like hope.

The villa terrace had been transformed into something straight out of a travel magazine. Candles flickered in small glass jars; the sea breeze carried the scent of rosemary and sea salt, and the table was set with rustic elegance. It was the kind of dinner that should have felt relaxing. Instead, tension crackled like static electricity under every fork.

Noah carried out a steaming pot of rabbit stew and placed it gently in the center of the table. Belinda refused to look directly at him, which meant she absolutely saw every move he made out of the corner of her eye. Carla grinned like a shark who smelled gossip. Jason, meanwhile, watched the dynamic with growing suspicion. His mother and the chef had shared about seventeen awkward glances already, and dinner had barely begun. It was obvious there was some history here.

'So, Noah,' he said casually, spooning stew into his bowl. 'How long have you known my mom?'

Belinda froze mid-sip.

Noah cleared his throat. 'Since we were kids, actually.'

Carla pounced eagerly. 'Oh yes. They were very close. Young hearts, summer nights, raging hormones.' Belle kicked her under the table so hard a spoon rattled while Jason choked on his stew. Carla didn't even flinch. 'What? That's how babies are made, Jason.'

Jason choked again, this time on his wine. Noah's ears turned scarlet. 'We were just friends,' he insisted quickly. 'Really good friends.'

'Uh-huh,' Carla drawled. 'And now you're, what was that phrase you used, Belinda? Just good friends who occasionally kiss?' Belle's head snapped toward her like she was considering murder.

Jason stared. 'Kissing? On vacation?'

Belle sputtered. 'It was… we were. There was a picnic! And waves, and sunstroke is a real medical condition!'

'Aha,' Jason nodded like a detective closing in on a suspect. 'So you are into this guy, the chef.'

'I ate the chef's picnic. That is not a euphemism,' Belinda hissed into her napkin. Noah coughed, wishing for spontaneous teleportation.

Carla leaned back, looking smug. 'I'm just saying, if my mother kissed a hot chef on a boat in Malta, I'd call that a good life choice.'

Jason blinked slowly. 'Carla, you're the same age as my mom. Do you really think this is appropriate behaviour?'

'Age is but a number,' she declared dramatically, then turned back to Noah with a wink. 'Tell him, Romeo.' Belinda inhaled deeply through her nose, then smiled too sweetly at Carla.

'If you do not stop talking, I will tell Jason about the ghost.'

Carla looked aghast. 'You wouldn't.'

'Oh, I would.'

Silence fell, blessed, glorious silence, broken only by a dog barking in the distance at absolutely nothing. Jason looked between Belinda and Noah one more time, eyebrows high. 'So, are we pretending nothing happened?' Carla asked, 'or pretending you're not both thinking about it happening again?'

Belinda stabbed a carrot with unnecessary force; Jason looked horrified. Noah rubbed the back of his neck, picked up the empty bread basket and scuttled back inside.

Carla clapped her hands in glee. 'I love family dinners.'

Chapter Twenty-Six

They got through dinner with stilted conversation. Jason kept looking at her like he didn't recognise her anymore. Noah, the consummate professional, kept the amazing food coming and his thoughts to himself. When he began to clear the empty dishes, Belinda picked up a couple of plates and followed him into the kitchen. Now they stood shoulder-to-shoulder in the villa's warm kitchen, the tension between them more palpable than the steam rising from the sink. 'I'm sorry about dinner,' Belle murmured, putting the plates on the side. 'Carla should come with a warning label.'

Noah chuckled under his breath; a flash of a smile crossed his face. 'I thought it was… entertaining.'

'You have a high tolerance for embarrassment then,' she replied, trying not to stare at the way his forearms flexed while scrubbing a pan. He glanced over, eyes soft.

'I didn't mind, honestly.'

Her heart fluttered in a way she absolutely did not approve of. She opened her mouth, an apology on her lips, but footsteps interrupted. Jason stood in the doorway looking less than pleased. He coughed. 'I just came, just came to get some more wine,' he said, glancing around quickly, eyes alighting on the wine fridge. He made a big show of studying the bottles, pulling out this one and then that. When he couldn't drag it out any longer, he selected one and looked at it. 'I'll just take this out; are you coming, Mom?'

'I'll be there in a moment, Jason,' she said softly, smiling at his protectiveness, however wrongly placed. When he left, she turned to Noah. 'I wanted to apologise for not answering your message earlier; there was a lot going on.'

'Ah, yes. The long story.'

'Yes, definitely that. But also, I didn't know what to say.'

Carla clomped past the doorway, stuck her head into the kitchen, 'I'm just off to the toilet; don't let me disturb you two!' And laughing loudly, she carried on down the hall.

'I really should be better at ignoring her,' Belle groaned, her face flushing an adorable shade of pink.

'Please don't,' Noah replied. 'If she hadn't meddled, we never would've ended up on that boat.' She smiled despite herself. He looked at her properly, intensely, like he was memorising every line of her face. 'About the kisses,' he said, voice low. 'I'd really like there to be more of them.'

Belinda's breath caught in her throat. Her heart thudded a warning of danger, but her body whispered yes. 'Noah, we can't. This is crazy. I mean, yes, the kissing was nice.'

'Just nice?' he grinned.

'Okay then, the kissing was amazing. But I'm just here for a while, recently divorced and have no idea what I am doing…' she trailed off. He stepped closer, the scent of him invading her senses, and gently brushed a strand of hair from her cheek.

'Then I should make sure it's worth your while,' he murmured. And kissed her slowly, confidently, a promise he poured straight into her mouth. The kind of kiss that made her forget every reason she had to resist. When they finally pulled apart, Belinda whispered, almost breathless,

'Noah… what are we doing?'

He rested his forehead against hers. 'Something we should've done years ago.'

She looked into his beautiful green eyes and saw nothing but sincerity and promises of what could come next. Maybe she could trust this man.

'I'm still not interrupting you two,' Carla called as she walked back out to the terrace.

Belinda laughed, suddenly feeling that anything was possible. 'Let's meet tomorrow, and, well, talk, I guess.' She looked thoughtful for a moment. 'Annalise arrives mid-morning, so if our chef could make us lunch, maybe he'll have time to meet a friend later in the day?'

'He could definitely do that, especially if it was a good friend who kissed him occasionally.'

When Belinda went to bed that night, she was grinning, holding in the secret of their meeting tomorrow afternoon. There was no way she was telling Carla, not yet. And Jason obviously wasn't ready to accept that his mother was a woman who liked to kiss handsome men occasionally. She was barely ready to accept it, but it seemed like that was who she was now. It was completely insane; there was no way it could lead to anything, but she couldn't help herself. Noah was kind, caring, incredibly gorgeous and a fantastic kisser. It was a package too good to ignore. Wasn't it?

Her phone chimed, and she saw that an email had just arrived. She ignored the now-daily voice note notifications from Mike and scanned the email instead. The words written there knocked thoughts of tempting secret assignations clean out of her mind.

Chapter Twenty-Seven

'Susan?' Carla yelped over the breakfast table, nearly sloshing her orange juice down her silk kaftan. 'As in sister Susan. Sister Susan, whom you haven't seen in years, is coming here?'

'It appears that way,' Belinda replied, trying not to gaze at Noah while he laid out their breakfast fare. Fresh fruit glistening like jewels in the morning sun, coffee steaming invitingly. 'She gets in this evening.'

'Well, that's a turn-up for the books. This holiday is getting more interesting by the day!'

Belinda sighed into her coffee, trying not to let her nerves choke her. 'I know. I honestly did not expect her to even respond, let alone hop on a plane. We've hardly exchanged two sentences in ten years.'

'Where's she gonna sleep?'

Belinda paused, pressed her hand to her forehead, a look of consternation on her face. 'God, I hadn't even thought about that. I guess she'll have to bunk in with me until Jason leaves. Although she didn't say how long she was coming for. Or why, for that matter.'

Carla sighed happily, savoring the drama like a box of chocolates. 'I have to say you're the best friend a girl could have. Laying on all this entertainment for me. Kissing hot chefs, a son with a secretive wife. And we've yet to meet Annalise's latest, which should be fun.'

'I doubt that very much,' Jason grumbled as he emerged, hair rumpled, eyes still half-asleep. He flopped gracelessly into a chair. 'What's his name anyway?'

'Jake something,' said Belinda, scrolling through her email, 'I think that's what her confirmation said.'

'Flaky Jake, the nickname just writes itself.'

Belinda shot him a maternal warning look. 'I need you to promise me you'll be nice, Jason. I know your sister's tastes in partners have been a little odd over the years but she sounds very keen on this one, so let's give him a chance, ok?' Jason didn't answer but did grunt in a way that sounded vaguely agreeable.

Just then Noah appeared, sliding down a plate of ricotta-stuffed pastizzi with a smile bright enough to power the entire island. 'So, I gather it's going to be a full house for breakfast tomorrow?'

'Sure is, hun, we're going to keep you busy, that's for sure,' Carla winked at him.

Noah gave her a playful salute. 'Maybe I'll have to get the ghost, I mean Magda, in to help with service then,' he replied with a grin, and turned to get them more coffee. Belinda choked back a laugh at the look of outrage on Carla's face.

'That man is getting too cocky by half!' she huffed. 'You can go off a person, you know,' she shouted at his retreating back.

When Annalise arrived, the villa doors flew open like the final act of a Broadway musical. 'Mom!' Annalise squealed, dress swishing around her like a blooming peony. She dashed forward, collapsing into Belinda's arms with kisses on both cheeks. The air filled with the scent of jasmine and the sound of her many bangles sliding up her arms. 'This place is fabulous, I'm so happy to be here!' She spun in a delighted circle before calling down the hallway to where her travelling companion was obviously tipping the driver. 'Hurry up, Jakey, I want to introduce you to everyone.'

Jason braced himself like a man preparing for battle. But the man who walked into the lounge, with an open friendly smile on his chiseled face, was tall, broad-shouldered and wearing what looked like an Armani suit that probably cost more than a car. There was a beat of silence as they all stared at him. 'You must be Belinda,' he said, stretching out his hand and pumping hers. 'Your daughter obviously gets her good looks from you.'

'Smooth,' muttered Jason, then did a double take, his eyes widening as he looked at him. 'You're Jake Medina,' he exclaimed, looking at him in awe. 'CEO of Morgan and Wiseman.'

Jake laughed modestly. 'Guilty as charged. And you must be Jason. Annalise has told me all about you.'

'Not so flaky now,' Carla nudged him playfully, eyebrows lifted somewhere close to her hairline. Morgan and Wiseman was one of the biggest financial institutions in the world, and this guy was the hotshot that had got them there. This was definitely going to be interesting.

Noah paused in the archway, holding a fresh pot of coffee and absolutely not spying. Except he totally was. He'd heard the squeals, the excitement and the jasmine-perfumed whirlwind. And now here he was, watching Belle's daughter cling to her like a returning movie star, while her Very Unexpected Boyfriend shook hands like a man used to closing multi-million-euro deals before breakfast. Jake Medina, the infamous CEO of Morgan & Wiseman. A man whose watch probably cost more than Noah's entire house.

Noah cleared his throat lightly, though nobody noticed. He could feel his shirt, which had seemed perfectly sensible five minutes ago, now clinging awkwardly to his shoulders. Had he spilled flour on himself earlier? Probably. Wonderful. Jake turned toward him just as he stepped forward. 'Hello there,' Jake said warmly, offering a firm handshake. 'Jake Medina.'

Noah wiped his palm discreetly on his apron before shaking back. 'Noah Caruana, chef.' He instantly wanted to slam his head against the wall. Chef. As if Jake couldn't guess from the telltale apron covered in flour and the coffeepot.

Jake's smile broadened, all effortless confidence. 'Excellent. I've heard the food here is incredible. I look forward to confirming that personally.'

Noah smiled back, or at least arranged his lips into something smile-adjacent, then turned to Belle, who was watching the interaction very closely, teeth sunk into her bottom lip like she was nervous he might… what? Challenge the billionaire to a duel? The thought made him want to laugh. Or throw up. Hard to be sure. 'Coffee?' he offered, a little too brightly. He poured for everyone, only spilling a tiny bit when Jake flashed another one of those polished smiles, and set the pot down gently. Carla, never one to leave an awkward moment alone, leaned forward with a wolfish glint in her eye.

'So, Jake,' she purred, 'how long are you two staying?'

Jake glanced affectionately at Annalise. 'Not sure yet.

We're taking some time off, enjoying life. Seeing where things lead.'

Belle's eyes flicked to Noah. And for the tiniest moment, there it was — that spark they'd shared. The one that made him feel like a man standing on the edge of something new. But then she looked away, and she laughed at something Jake said. And Noah felt that spark wobble dangerously. He exhaled, trying to school his expression into neutrality. She has a life. A wealthy, well-connected, Armani-suit-wearing life.

And you… you chop onions for a living. Max would have disagreed. Dogs care nothing for Armani, but Max wasn't here to argue the point with his owner. Belle looked his way again and gave a small, shy smile. And just like that, he was done for. Completely done for. He saw Carla staring at them, a delighted smirk on her face, so with a polite nod, Noah retreated toward the kitchen. Because if he stayed another second, he was pretty sure Carla would air his romantic feelings out loud for the entire villa to judge.

Back behind the safety of his pans and simmering sauces, Noah muttered to himself. 'Well… this just got complicated.' Here he was falling in love again with a girl that he used to know, but she wasn't the same girl. She was a beautiful, smart, sophisticated woman who was used to the luxuries in life. What could he offer her apart from a decent plate of pasta and an excitable dog?

Chapter Twenty-Eight

The morning market in Valletta was already in full swing, with the loud bargaining, the scent of fresh bread and basil, the clatter of crates. Noah weaved through the bustle; a basket hooked over one elbow. He spotted Mikiel near his usual spot, weighing fish with the slow, practiced care of a man who had opinions about his produce and would absolutely state them at volume.

'Morning, old man,' Noah said, trying, and failing, to sound casual.

Mikiel looked up. 'You've got a face like a man who is in love or deeply constipated.'

'Thanks,' Noah muttered. 'Things are complicated.'

'Ah. In love.' Mikiel grinned, thrusting a salmon into his hand and nodding approvingly when Noah put it in his basket. 'So. Belle.'

Noah blinked. 'Why would you assume it's Belle?'

Mikiel snorted loudly enough to turn heads. 'Because you look like a man who's spent all night thinking about a woman. And it's been a long time since you've looked at a woman like that, why do you think I sent you out on the boat?'

Noah's chest tightened. He scuffed a shoe against the cobblestones. 'It's just, she's from another world, you know? Fancy. Successful. The kind of woman who vacations in luxury villas with infinity pools and billionaires suddenly showing up for breakfast.'

Mikiel raised a shaggy brow. 'And you?'

'I'm just a chef,' Noah said. 'Barely scraping by. Working summer jobs. Living in a small house held together by paint and prayer.'

Mikiel grabbed him by the shoulders, firm and fatherly. 'Listen to me, boy. You feed people joy. You make them feel alive again and appreciate nature's bounty. Do you think that's small?' His voice softened. 'Love doesn't care about bank accounts. And a woman doesn't chase a man's money when she already has her own, in my experience.'

Noah swallowed, throat tight. 'But her life is in America and mine is here. What if I open my heart… and she leaves? Again.'

Mikiel tapped his chest with a thick finger. 'Better a heart cracked open by love than one sealed shut by fear.' Then he shoved a packet of prawns into Noah's basket. 'Also, I've seen the way she looks at you. The way Sarah used to. Don't be an idiot.'

Noah laughed, surprised and stung and hopeful all at once. 'You always know exactly what to say, old man.'

'Of course I do. I'm very wise,' Mikiel said, already turning to yell at a tourist who dared to poke at his fish the wrong way. 'And very humble.' Noah shook his head, smiling as he headed off toward the vegetable stalls. Maybe Mikiel was right. Maybe this wasn't something to run from.

Maybe… it was something to fight for.

The kitchen smelled like the sea had decided to flirt with everyone's tastebuds as he prepared lunch. Noah set the fresh salmon on the chopping block, his knife gliding through the pink flesh with practiced ease. The bowl of plump prawns sat nearby, tails curled as if they were giggling about secrets. Mikiel's sage advice still echoed in his chest: better a heart cracked open by love…

Noah seasoned the fish with lemon, oil, and cracked pepper, forcing his breathing into something resembling normal. He had sent the message, *Wine later?* and against every panicked nerve in his body, Belle had responded with a simple: *Yes. I'd love to.*

He only read it twelve times. When he stepped onto the terrace to set the table, she was already there, laughing at something Jason had said, sunglasses tipping down her nose, curls catching the sunlight like it adored her. Noah's heart did a weird flip, like a fish tossed back into the sea. She caught him looking, and her lips curved. Just slightly. Enough to send heat washing up his neck. He pretended the cutlery he was laying was suddenly extremely fascinating. Back inside, thoughts all over the place, he tossed prawns into a sizzling pan of garlic and butter. They hissed and curled, and Noah swallowed hard.

'You okay there, chef?' Carla's voice drifted in from the doorway, far too smug for this early in the day.

'Perfectly fine,' he replied, almost snapping a prawn tail in half.

Carla sauntered over like a cat who'd seen the cream, the cow, and the dairy farmer blushing. 'Just checking. You look a little flushed.'

'It's warm by the stove,' he muttered.

'Mm-hmm.' Her knowing chuckle trailed behind her as she returned outside. Not much escaped her notice, and she'd seen the furtive glances between Belinda and the hot chef enough to know their story wasn't over yet. At least she hoped for her friend's sake it wasn't, that girl was due a man who looked at her like she lit up his world.

He plated everything with a flourish, seared salmon atop a bright salad dotted with capers, prawns nestled like golden jewels, a drizzle of olive oil pooling like liquid sunshine. The kind of meal that looked effortless but had his nerves seasoned into every bite. When he carried the dishes out, Belle sat straighter in her seat, but her eyes didn't leave his. For a moment, the world shrank to two people and a table between them.

Then Jason asked loudly, trying to impress Jake, if the prawns were organic, and the spell shattered. 'If you want them to be,' Noah shot back without thinking, and Belle nearly snorted water out of her nose. Lunch continued as a ridiculous dance of stolen glances. Her sandal brushed his foot when he leaned to refill her water; a spark skittered up his spine. She murmured thank you, voice barely above a whisper just for him, eyes saying far more than words dared.

When the plates were emptied and everyone stretched back in their chairs, Annalise announced that she and Jake were going for a walk. Carla, sensing an opportunity to throw the lovebirds together again, dragged Jason inside with her to plan birthday festivities for tomorrow. Leaving Belinda and Noah alone in the warm hush.

She looked at him, soft but uncertain. 'So,' she said lightly, the corner of her mouth curving, 'about that wine?'

Noah's heart expanded in his chest like a sail filling with wind. 'I was hoping you'd say that,' he said. And just like that, his afternoon had a purpose far better than freshly painted walls.

Chapter Twenty-Nine

Belinda spent far too long choosing a dress for someone who absolutely wasn't trying to impress the chef. She told herself it was because Malta was warm and she needed something comfortable. That a sundress with thin straps and a sweep of floral print was totally practical. That the adding of lip gloss was merely because her lips were dry. And the faint perfume was… mosquito repellent. Yes, obviously. She rolled her eyes at her own reflection. *Get a grip, woman.*

Noah knew about a tiny café tucked right into the harbour wall, whitewashed, with uneven blue tables and chairs that looked stolen from a postcard, and that's where he suggested they meet. Belinda arrived a few minutes early, blaming jet lag for her eagerness. The salty breeze pressed soft waves against the quay, fishing boats bobbing like lazy ducks in the late afternoon sun.

When she spotted Noah approaching from inside, carrying a bottle of chilled wine and two glasses by their stems, her heart executed a cartwheel. His hair was still damp from his afternoon shower, shirt sleeves pushed up his forearms, revealing strong, sun-browned skin dusted lightly with dark hair. Of all the ridiculous things to find attractive…

He smiled when he reached her. 'Hey.'

'Hi.' She was proud the word didn't come out as a squeak.

'I thought we could watch the boats coming in,' he said, glancing to the horizon where a ragtag fleet of fishing vessels nudged toward the harbour. 'It's not the villa terrace, but I like it here.'

'It's perfect,' she said, looking around, and meant it.

He poured the wine, and they clinked glasses before settling into their seats. The tang of sea air mixed with citrus and oregano drifting from the café kitchen, pure Mediterranean magic. A few beats of silence stretched between them, comfortable yet charged.

'So,' Belle started. 'About the other day.'

'Right,' Noah rubbed the back of his neck. 'The boat. The kisses.'

She tucked a strand of hair behind her ear, pretending to examine a gondola-shaped souvenir menu holder. 'Yes, that.'

'We said friends,' Noah reminded softly. 'But I don't think either of us acted very… friendly.'

Belle laughed nervously. 'No. We were terrible at it.'

His smile warmed. 'Do you want to try again? At the friendship part?'

She lifted her eyes, and something in his expression — hopeful, careful — melted her. 'I want…' she hesitated, searching for bravery she rarely used, 'whatever this is. Even if we're terrible at it.'

His face lit with quiet relief. 'Good. I was hoping you'd say that.'

A fishing boat horn sounded, and a crewman shouted something cheerful in Maltese. Noah leaned forward a little, not close enough to kiss her, but close enough that her pulse fluttered like a trapped bird.

Belinda exhaled a laugh. 'We really are awful at uncomplicated things.'

'Then let's be complicated together.' He raised his glass, waiting for hers to meet it.

She tapped it gently with a smile. 'To terrible friends.'

'To terrible friends,' he agreed, eyes promising something much more. And above them, gulls swooped and cried, as if applauding a beginning neither of them could quite name yet.

The afternoon slipped through Belinda's fingers like sea-sprayed sunlight, warm, brilliant, impossible to hold on to. She and Noah talked and laughed and shared stories that felt both too personal and not personal enough, as though each was trying to learn the other by heart without letting on. Eventually, she checked her phone.

'Oh no,' she gasped. 'I'm supposed to meet my sister at the villa when she arrives.'

Noah blinked, as though returning from a pleasant dream. 'Sister? The mysterious, unexpected one?'

'The very same.' Belinda stood up, grabbing her bag. 'She's probably at the door right now wondering if she's made a huge mistake.'

He chuckled and reached for her hand as they walked toward the waterfront path. Each step was a delicious contradiction. She wanted to hurry, and she desperately wanted to slow down.

'I had a really good time,' he said once they stopped

beside a sun-bleached wall blooming with pink bougainvillea.

'Me too,' she breathed. 'Maybe too good.'

'Dangerously good,' he said with a playful seriousness, the grin she loved so much making an appearance. She glanced toward the street leading inland. Responsibility tugged one direction; Noah tugged the other. And for once, she let her heart win. She rose on her toes and pressed a quick, sweet kiss to his lips. Somehow it wasn't quick at all. His hand came to her waist. The breeze lifted her hair. Time stalled like an overdramatic soap opera. When they finally parted, they were both smiling like fools.

'I should…'

'Yeah, go,' he finished softly. They stood there for another beat, not moving. Then Belinda turned, laughing at her own reluctance. She waved once as she hurried off, her sundress fluttering behind her. Noah watched until she rounded the corner, happiness settling in the lines of his face.

Neither of them noticed the figure frozen just beyond the railings, Annalise, sunglasses perched atop her head, jaw dangling in pure cinematic horror. Mom. Kissing. The chef. Her eyes widened further as comprehension struck. 'This is not the plan, not at all!' she whispered to herself. And with dramatic speed worthy of an Oscar, Annalise spun on her heel, already thinking how she could throw things off track so her surprise for tomorrow wouldn't be ruined.

Chapter Thirty

Belinda burst through the villa's front door, breathless and trying to look as though she'd merely stepped out for something respectable. The scent of jasmine and new arrivals was thick in the air. Susan was already standing in the lounge, arms folded, mouth pursed, a suitcase positioned like a defensive barricade. Same perfectly pressed bob, same disapproving eyebrow that could slice granite.

'Well,' Susan said, voice dripping ice, 'nice of you to finally show up.'

Belinda halted, heat still glowing on her lips from Noah's goodbye. 'I—I'm sorry, I lost track of time.'

'Doing what?' Susan snapped. 'Or should I say who?'

Belinda blinked. 'Excuse me?'

Carla suddenly appeared at Belinda's elbow like a gremlin who thrives on drama. 'Oh, come on,' she purred. 'You know exactly what she means; we've had time for a little chat.' Belinda shot her a warning look. Carla ignored it with the grace of a rhinoceros in stilettos. 'I mean,' Carla continued, turning to Susan, 'she was obviously out kissing the hot chef again. Honestly, it's about time she got back in the saddle.'

Belinda gasped. 'Carla!'

'Oh, please,' Susan scoffed, eyes widening to full moral superiority mode. 'Isn't this a little irresponsible? You just got divorced, Belinda.'

'And you just arrived,' Belinda retorted, planting her hands on her hips. 'You don't get to swoop back into my life and start judging my choices before you've even had a glass of the welcome prosecco.'

Carla, eyes shining with mischief, raised her hand. 'I'll get the prosecco. This is getting good.'

Susan ignored her. 'I'm simply concerned,' she went on, with the tone of someone who had never been 'simply' anything in her life. 'Running around with a… a staff member? You can't seriously think that's appropriate.'

Belinda took a deep breath, the kind you take before doing something brave or stupid. 'His name is Noah,' she said, calmer now. 'And he's kind, and funny, and he makes me feel like I matter again. So no, I don't care if he's a chef. Or if you think it's a bad idea. You haven't been around to care about anything in my life for years, Susan.'

Susan faltered, only for a breath, but Belinda saw it. A tiny crack in the frost. 'I flew here to fix things,' Susan whispered stiffly. 'Not to fight.' Belinda softened, despite herself. Carla, however, was already topping up her glass like this was prime-time television.

'Then maybe,' she said, 'we start by not throwing shade at the first nice thing that's happened to me in a long time.' Susan looked away, blinking too quickly.

Carla ushered them toward the terrace table as though directing actors onstage. A tray already waited there, prosecco poured, olives glistening, cushions plumped. Carla lived for moments like this. Belinda sat first, pulse still fluttering from… well, everything. Susan took the seat opposite her with that rigid poise she'd perfected over decades, like a queen who found the throne uncomfortable but refused to shift an inch. Carla plopped into the third chair, elbows on the table, ready for the show.

'So,' Belinda began gently, 'how have you been, Sue?' Susan's fingers twisted around her glass stem. Not a good sign, Susan never fidgeted. Ever.

'I suppose,' she began coolly, 'I should tell you right away Gerald died.'

The universe seemed to hold its breath. 'Oh, Susan…' Belinda reached out automatically, her chest squeezing. Susan waved the condolences away with a curt flap of her hand, as though swatting a fly.

'No, no, don't. Really. It was a relief.' Carla's prosecco paused halfway to her mouth. Now they were talking. Susan inhaled, and something fragile flickered in her gaze. 'Gerald was, well. You remember how particular he could be.'

'Particular?' Belinda repeated. 'He once sent my Christmas card back because the handwriting was "too childish."' Carla spluttered with delight.

'It was a ballpoint pen,' Susan muttered defensively. 'But yes. That was… one of his many uncompromising standards.' She stared out toward the sea. 'He didn't like me talking to you. Or anyone, really. He said family distracted me from my responsibilities. Visiting Mother when she was dying turned into World War III. I barely made it to the funeral.'

Belinda's heart cracked right open. 'Why didn't you tell me?'

'He monitored everything,' Susan said, voice tight. 'My emails, my phone, once he stood behind me while I wrote a message to you and dictated what I should say. You stopped trying after a while because I always cancelled plans. And… I let you think it was me.'

Carla's eyes were as big as the olives on the table. 'Sweet baby Jesus,' she whispered. 'He was a full-blown bastard.'

A tiny laugh, small, surprised, escaped Susan. 'Yes. He really was.' Belinda reached across the table again, slower this time. Susan let her take her hand.

'I thought you didn't care,' she murmured.

'I cared very much,' Susan said. 'I just didn't know how to break free.'

Carla sniffed dramatically and raised her glass. 'To breaking free, preferably somewhere with sun-loungers and hot men.'

Susan's lips twitched with the ghost of a smile. 'To freedom,' she agreed quietly, clinking her glass.

Belinda squeezed her hand. 'You're safe now. Back with family, with me.'

Susan blinked rapidly again, then straightened her shoulders. 'Don't get sentimental. I might cry and ruin my mascara.'

Carla leaned in with a wicked grin. 'Oh, honey, if you think today's emotional, wait until you hear what your niece and nephew have been up to.' Belinda groaned into her prosecco as Susan's brows shot up and Carla, delighted, topped everyone's glasses again.

Drama, after all, was best served with bubbles.

Chapter Thirty-One

The restaurant organised by Sophia, the concierge, for them that night was perched on the edge of Valletta's old bastions, the stone walls glowing gold in the evening sun and the harbour stretched beneath them like spilled ink dotted with lights. It was the kind of place where waiters glided rather than walked and the water glasses refilled themselves as if by magic.

Belinda should have been soaking in every detail, the beauty, the history, the laughter of loved ones around her, but all she could think about was Noah's hands brushing hers as he'd passed her the wine that afternoon. The quick, secret kiss that still tingled on her lips. His smile when he'd said he wanted to see her again. And now she sat here trying to pretend she wasn't wildly, ridiculously smitten. Get a grip, she scolded herself, smiling politely at the waiter. This can't be a thing. It's too soon. Too complicated. Too… wonderful? No. Stop it.

Across the table, Susan gave her a sideways look. 'You appear distracted.'

'Oh?' Belinda chirped too brightly. 'I'm just admiring the architecture.'

'You're facing the kitchen,' Susan replied flatly.

Carla snickered over her martini. Jason, meanwhile, was peppering Jake with breathless questions about mergers and acquisitions like a golden retriever who'd learned to talk. 'And how did you negotiate that takeover? The press said it was impossible, but you did it!'

Jake clapped him on the shoulder, flawless teeth flashing. 'Oh, you know. Sometimes the thing that seems impossible just requires a leap of faith.'

Belinda paused because Jake had said it with the exact same gentle confidence Noah used when he'd convinced her to get in the water on Manoel Island. Her heart did that boing thing again. Carla leaned closer and whispered, 'you're thinking about him.'

Belinda nearly inhaled her wine. 'Carla!' she hissed

'What? I can practically hear you swooning. It sounds like wind chimes and heavy breathing.'

Annalise, sitting beside them, narrowed her eyes, eagle-like, calculating. 'Who's swooning?' She asked lightly, stabbing a prawn a little too hard.

'Your mother,' Carla answered, utterly unhelpful. 'Over the hot chef.'

Annalise's fork froze mid-air, then her lips curved into her sweetest, fakest PR-polished smile. 'Oh,' she said. 'That chef.'

Belinda felt like crawling under the table. 'We are not discussing this.'

'No?' Carla asked innocently. 'But it's such rich material.' Even Susan smirked at that. Dessert arrived, honeyed ġelat and tiny pastries that melted on the tongue, and the conversation spiraled on. Belinda tried to pay attention, but she glanced toward the harbour and imagined Noah, sleeves rolled, laughing as he kneaded dough or chopped herbs, unaware he'd taken up full-time residence in her thoughts. Her phone buzzed in her lap, Noah.

Hope dinner is lovely. Thought of you when I saw the moon tonight.

She swallowed a stupidly giddy laugh. Carla saw the look on her face and kicked her under the table gently, in excitement. Annalise saw it too, and her eyes sharpened. Oh boy, Carla thought, watching Annalise's expression darken into plotting mode. This holiday just got even better. And Belinda, blissfully unaware of the silent rivalry brewing mere inches from her, secretly typed back beneath the tablecloth.

Me too.

Sunlight streamed through the villa's breakfast terrace the next morning, catching dust motes and making everything look far too idyllic for the emotional minefield currently present. It danced across whitewashed walls, birds chirped, and a gentle sea breeze wafted through, as if the world itself was celebrating someone turning fifty today.

Noah arrived first, wheeling out a trolley laden with platters, warm ftira rolls, fresh fruit, honeycomb dripping golden threads, scrambled eggs with herbs from the villa garden. He tried to focus on the food, but his heart was already halfway across the terrace, scanning for her.

Belinda stepped out a moment later. She wasn't even trying to be dramatic — a simple sundress, hair caught up messily — but Noah forgot how breathing worked for a very unprofessional second. She gave him a small, shy smile. The kind that said: Yes, yesterday happened. And yes, I liked it too. Before either could speak, Carla appeared like the herald of chaos.

'Well, happy birthday, fifty-and-fabulous!' she declared, hugging Belinda and smirking shamelessly at Noah. 'You look suspiciously well-rested for someone nearing pension age.'

Belinda turned the colour of a ripe strawberry and nudged her. 'Carla,' she hissed. 'Sit down. Quietly.'

Carla did neither of those things, but she reached for the coffee, which at least halved the risk of additional commentary. Jason trudged in next, hair askew, groaning like sleep had personally betrayed him. He spotted Jake already checking emails and sat beside him as reverently as a monk beside a saint. 'You're up early,' Jason said, impressed.

'Habit,' Jake replied, smiling warmly. 'Markets never sleep. Also, Annalise snores.'

'I do not,' Annalise snapped, gliding in behind them, sunglasses perched like armour. She placed a perfectly delicate kiss on Jake's cheek. Then she looked at Belinda, and then at Noah, and her smile sharpened like manicure scissors. 'Morning,' she said silkily. 'Busy day for you, isn't it? Running after… guests.' She made guests sound like a contagious disease.

Belinda stared fixedly at her orange juice. Susan arrived last, looking surprisingly refreshed and faintly amused. 'So,' she said, pouring herself the tea that she preferred, 'I gather we're all going on a yacht today to celebrate the big birthday. I can't remember the last time I did something so decadent.'

'Probably when Gerald insisted you organise that fundraiser on a boat,' Carla offered. 'The one where he criticised the water for being too wavy.'

Susan snorted into her cup, a sound that suggested she was rapidly shedding decades of marital repression. Noah cleared his throat, professional mode activated. 'Your driver will pick you up in an hour to take you to the marina. You'll sail out past Comino and then onto Gozo. And of course, I will be here tonight for dinner service.' He glanced at Belle; she glanced back, and her toes curled in her sandals. Annalise noticed and frowned hard enough to age a year.

'Well,' Jake announced, folding his napkin with CEO decisiveness. 'A day on the water is exactly what we all need. Relaxation, sunshine, and family time, right?' He placed a charming arm around Annalise, who continued glaring at the Belle & Noah Show.

Belinda forced a breezy smile and stood. 'I'll just grab my bag.'

Annalise watched her go, plotting silently as Noah gathered stray plates, pretending not to watch Belle's retreating form, pretending not to feel like gravity itself tugged whenever she walked away. Carla leaned over to him. 'Don't mess this up,' she whispered gleefully. 'I have invested heavily in this romance.' He flushed, smiled, and tried to hide how hopeful he suddenly felt. The day had barely begun, and already the spark between them was brighter than the Maltese sun.

Chapter Thirty-Two

Noah stacked the last of the drained coffee cups on the counter, trying to ignore the tiny spark of anticipation flickering in his chest. Today was Belinda's birthday, and he wanted to make it special. Not just professionally. In a please-let-this-become-something-real way. He rinsed a platter of pastry flakes into the bin, humming under his breath, mentally planning the dinner prep once they left for the boat. The kitchen door opened without warning.

'Oh!' he said, startled as Annalise strode inside like she owned the place. 'Everything all right?'

'I just wanted to say thank you,' she replied sweetly, too sweetly. Like a cupcake laced with arsenic. 'For looking after Mom while she's been… sorting things out.'

He nodded, relieved. 'Of course. She deserves a break.'

A little "hm" slipped out of Annalise, not approval, more like mild disgust disguised as politeness. 'Yes. A break, before everything gets back on track,' she said, picking up a strawberry and examining it like she expected it to confess.

'She and my dad have been talking a lot lately. About reconciliation and, you know, fixing their marriage.'

His grip tightened around the cloth. 'Oh?'

'Yes, they've been texting and calling a lot while she's been here.' Annalise picked up one of the perfectly polished dessert spoons, studying her reflection in it. 'Dad is actually flying out today.' She let that hang a beat too long. 'To join us on the boat. Birthday surprise!'

Noah's heart dropped somewhere near his shoes, his pulse thudding in his ears. 'I… I didn't know that,' he managed.

'Oh, you know how relationships are,' Annalise sighed dramatically, brushing imaginary dust off her manicure. 'Sometimes people just need a little space to remember what they really want.' A beat. 'And Mom always wanted Dad. You know how love is.'

He didn't. Not anymore.

'Dad's the love of her life,' she continued, twisting the knife with a bright, unbothered smile. 'She never really stopped loving him. And this trip made her realise that.'

Noah placed the cloth down carefully because the alternative was shredding it. 'Right,' he said softly. 'Of course.' He stared at the tiled floor. There it was, the truth he'd been too foolish to consider. Belinda had a whole life, a history, a family. A future that didn't include him. As the door clicked shut behind her, Noah exhaled shakily and leaned both hands on the counter, head bowed. His throat burned, and his stomach twisted.

Of course, he should have known. This was just a holiday fling, a convenient distraction before she went back to her world. Where she belonged. And he, a chef at a rental villa, would disappear like the last day of summer. He squared his shoulders, forcing the ache back down. He would have to protect what was left of his stupid heart. Checking the dishwasher to see if it was running, he glanced around the kitchen, and then walked out the door.

The yacht was a luxury catamaran, with three decks gleaming under the sunshine and chrome fixtures that reflected the soft turquoise of the sea. Crew members in crisp uniforms moved smoothly about, a well-choreographed dance of quiet service. Belinda paused to take it all in: the polished wood railings, the sweeping white sails just beginning to unfurl, the gentle sway promising adventure.

She slipped off her sandals and placed them in the wicker basket provided, feet sinking onto the cool teak deck. Fifty, she thought. This is a pretty spectacular way to turn fifty. If only Noah were here. Her gaze flicked automatically toward the marina they'd be leaving soon, disappointment tugging at her. But she'd see him tonight. That was something else to look forward to today.

They followed the hostess into the main saloon, a sun-drenched space of white leather seating and panoramic windows. A bottle of champagne was already popping, its foam catching the light in sparkling arcs before settling into flutes.

'Happy birthday, Belinda,' said a deep, all too familiar voice behind her.

The glass nearly slipped from her hand as she spun around. 'Mike! What are you doing here?' Her ex-husband stood there, annoyingly handsome in a navy blazer and that smug, amiable smile she'd once loved. In his hand was an enormous bouquet of red roses.

'Yes, Mike.' Carla appeared instantly at Belinda's side,

jaw set, posture like a guard dog about to bite. 'What exactly are you doing here?'

'I came to give you these,' Mike said cheerfully, extending the bouquet like an offer of peace. 'I thought today would be a good day for us to talk?'

Belinda recoiled. 'I have absolutely nothing to say to you, and you can stick those where the sun doesn't shine.'

'Mom!' Annalise gasped, her voice high with disbelief, looking between them like a spectator at a tennis match gone wrong. 'Why are you being like that?'

'I'm trying to fix things. It's what our daughter wanted.' He shot Annalise a grateful look that only made her shrink in her seat. Belinda felt the floor tilt, and not from the gentle rock of the yacht, but from pure fury.

'You manipulated our daughter into believing there's even a possibility of us getting back together?'

He hesitated, only for a breath, but it was enough. 'I didn't manipulate—'

Carla barked a laugh. 'You, Michael McGuire, manipulate oxygen when you breathe. Don't insult us.'

Annalise's eyes darted between her parents, cheeks reddening. 'Dad just said… you two had been talking. You said you were in touch again.'

Belinda swung toward her daughter, horrified. 'I texted him to tell him about a tax form and to stop sending me voice messages,' she snapped. 'That's not talking. That's damage control.'

Mike's smile slipped, irritation surfacing beneath the polished charm. 'Well, I thought maybe we could reset. Start again. You still look beautiful, Belinda.'

Belinda blinked at him slowly, in the way of a child holding a lit match. 'Compliments don't erase two decades of being taken for granted, Mike.'

He opened his mouth again, but Susan rose from her seat with surprising authority. 'That's enough.' Everyone turned. Her voice was steady, too steady, the kind that comes from surviving someone who shaped your every breath. 'You don't ambush a woman on her birthday cruise,' she said crisply. 'You don't show up uninvited, bearing roses like you're the hero of some damn romance novel. She said no. Respect it.'

Mike stared at her, thrown off balance. He didn't know this version of Susan, the one who no longer flinched. Jason cleared his throat. 'Honestly, Dad, this is not cool.'

Belinda swallowed hard. Thank God Noah didn't know about any of this. She steadied herself on the back of a leather seat. 'I want you off this boat,' she said quietly. Every head snapped toward her. 'Now.'

'But,'

'Now, Mike.'

A tense silence stretched as two crew members discreetly approached, ready to usher him to the gangplank. Mike set the roses on the table, a gesture meant to be noble, but it only looked pathetic. He tried again, softer this time. 'Belinda, I just wanted to fix things.'

'You should have fixed things years ago,' she replied.

Carla clapped a hand on Belinda's shoulder, proud as hell. 'Happy birthday to that,' she whispered.

As Mike stepped toward the exit, Annalise darted forward. 'Dad…' He kissed her forehead.

'I'll call you later.' And then he was gone, escorted down the ramp to the harbourside.

The moment he disappeared from view, the air in the saloon shifted, a collective exhale. Belinda sagged into a chair, rubbing her temples. 'God. What a mess!'

Carla reached for a champagne flute and thrust it into

her hand. 'To new beginnings,' she declared. 'And to never again letting a mediocre man ruin a luxury yacht experience.'

There was a smattering of relieved laughter. But one person wasn't laughing. Annalise sat rigidly, face pale, eyes narrowed with dawning horror as the truth settled in. She hadn't just miscalculated. She'd potentially destroyed the best chance her mother had to find a new happiness. What had she done?

Chapter Thirty-Three

Noah attacked the wooden shutter as if it had personally betrayed him. Sandpaper rasped furiously against flaking paint, the kind of aggressive DIY usually reserved for heartbreak and possibly televised home improvement challenges. Blue curls of old paint fluttered to the ground like sad confetti. Max lay nearby on an old blanket, watching every violent swipe with a worried tilt to his head. His ears pricked each time Noah muttered something under his breath, most of which were words Max rarely heard unless his human burnt something or cut his hand.

'I mean,' scrape, scrape, scrape, 'why even kiss me?' scrape, scrape, 'If she was just, what? Killing time before her husband swooped in like—like some returning hero?' SCRAAAAAPE. The sandpaper slipped, burning his knuckles. Noah hissed in pain, dropping the shutter with a clatter. Max bolted up, whined, and nudged his leg. Noah leaned against the wall and pressed his forehead to his forearm, breathing hard. 'She could have told me,' he said, voice low but ragged. Max pressed closer, tail wagging slowly, cautiously, ready to comfort but unsure how deeply involved he should be. Romance was a complicated business for humans; for dogs, it was mostly about sniffing and sharing snacks. Noah sank to the floor beside him.

'She said she was divorced.' His laugh was hollow. 'Guess there's divorced on paper and divorced in the heart, huh?' Max placed a paw squarely on Noah's thigh. A declaration: I am here but also, treat please. Noah scrubbed a hand through his hair.

'How do you trust anything after that?' Then, more quietly: 'How was I stupid enough to think she liked me that way?' Max gave a soft woof. The kind that said, you are a very good human; anyone with working eyes can see that. And also, about that treat? Noah's shoulders slumped.

'She could be on that yacht right now planning her second honeymoon.' The bitterness stung his tongue. 'And I'm here. Repainting bloody shutters.' He tossed the sandpaper aside and stared out the window, toward the blue strip of ocean visible beyond the rooftops. Somewhere out there, she was raising a glass, looking stunning and untouchable. 'Happy birthday, Belle,' he murmured bitterly. Max whined again and licked his chin.

Noah closed his eyes and let himself imagine, just for a second, that he'd gotten it all wrong. That she did want him. That he hadn't been misled and discarded. Just for a second. Then the second ended, and reality remained stubbornly intact. 'All right,' he sighed, pushing to his feet. 'Come on, Max. Let's go ruin more paint.' Max barked in full agreement. They went back to work — one heartbroken man, one loyal dog, trying to sand away feelings that refused to disappear.

Belinda stood at the rail with Carla, wind teasing loose strands of her hair, the fizz of champagne warming her chest. This should have been pure, unfiltered joy. Her 50th birthday, on a luxury yacht with her loved ones, the Mediterranean sparkling like a giant disco ball on the water. But her phone remained stubbornly, maddeningly silent in her hand.

'I can't believe he hasn't replied,' she muttered, squinting at the screen as though she could force a response into existence. 'It's been hours. Hours, Carla. I texted 'wish you were here' which, for me, is practically a declaration of undying love!' Carla clucked sympathetically and plucked the phone from her grip before Belinda threw it into the ocean.

'You're overthinking,' she said breezily. 'He's probably elbow-deep in your birthday feast. The man is a culinary genius; genius takes time. Also, ovens. Many ovens.'

Belinda chewed her lip. 'But what if he thought it was too forward? Or too needy? Or too,'

'Belinda.' Carla cut her off and placed both hands dramatically on her shoulders. 'You are a stunning woman in a fabulous dress on a yacht. No one here is thinking 'needy.' Except maybe Jason when the champagne runs out.' Belinda huffed out a laugh, but her gaze drifted back toward Valletta's receding skyline and the man somewhere beyond it who she desperately hoped was thinking of her.

A few feet behind them, Annalise hovered by the deck stairs, pretending to admire the view while eavesdropping with the grace of a giraffe on roller skates. Her nails clicked anxiously against her champagne glass. She adored her mother; she just didn't like anything that upset the fragile balance of their family narrative. But she'd have to admit to herself that her mother was ready to move on. That she should move on.

Belinda sighed, 'I just really want things with Noah to go well. Seeing Mike again actually reinforced that for me.'

Carla leaned an elbow on the polished stainless steel and smiled. 'It will all go perfectly. Tonight, there will be delicious food, more champagne, and absolutely no ex-husbands allowed anywhere near your personal space. Just a hot chef.'

Ahead of them, Gozo emerged like a promise, cliffs and coves glowing under the sun. Belinda reached a decision; she was going to make the most of this beautiful day with her favourite people around her. But tonight, she was going to let Noah know, in no uncertain terms, exactly how she felt about him.

Chapter Thirty-Four

They had a wonderful time that day, the kind of day that felt dipped in sunlight and sealed into memory. The catamaran glided into secluded bays around Gozo, where the water shifted from sapphire to turquoise to deep, secret green. Each stop was more beautiful than the previous one. The captain would drop anchor, and the sea would shimmer invitingly beneath them. Jason and Annalise instantly reverted to being ten years old, splashing each other with wild shrieks, dunking heads, and accusing one another of cheating in games that had no rules to begin with.

'Children,' Belinda muttered affectionately from the swim ladder, wringing water from her hair as the two of them chased each other around a giant inflatable paddleboard.

'That's one word for them,' Susan replied dryly, slipping into the water with surprising grace. 'Personally, I'd go with lunatics.'

Further out, Jason and Jake found a rocky outcrop that

became their personal arena. They climbed higher and higher with each leap into the water, sunlight bouncing off their shoulders. 'I'm telling you,' Jason puffed, wiping water from his eyes, 'this is at least a twenty-foot drop.'

Jake laughed, rolling his eyes. 'More like ten. But go on, prove you're the bravest.' Jason jumped, arms windmilling, followed by a victory roar that startled a flock of seabirds. Jake followed with the ease of a man who ran multinational corporations for breakfast and conquered cliffs for dessert. Jason pretended not to be impressed, but his grin told another story.

Lunch at a cliff-side restaurant came with views so stunning they made conversation pause. There were plates of fresh swordfish carpaccio, olives drenched in their own oil, crusty Maltese bread still warm from the oven, and crisp white wine that tasted like sea breeze and freedom. Belinda and Susan were tucked into a corner, leaning close and laughing, real, genuine laughter that made Belinda's heart feel lighter than it had in years.

'So, he actually banned Christmas music?' Belinda asked incredulously.

'For twenty-seven years,' Susan replied, deadpan. 'Said it was 'commercial nonsense.' I had to listen to Bing Crosby in the laundry room with headphones like a criminal.'

Belinda snorted so loudly that Carla, two tables away, glanced over mid–flirtation. Carla had singled out the handsome captain early. She twirled her straw in her drink while he gestured passionately about sailing routes, muscles shifting under his linen shirt like a living travel brochure. 'Oh yes,' she purred, 'please tell me more about port-side navigation.' She didn't understand a word, but she didn't need to.

With every hour, the sun-baked golden freckles onto

noses, hair dried into salty waves, and hearts, previously reluctant ones, loosened. Belinda looked out over the water, her chest full of warmth and laughter and the tiniest ache. She wished Noah could see her now. She wished she could see him.

It was a perfect day but with one perfect thing missing.

The sun dipped low behind the limestone skyline as the catamaran eased back toward Valletta, the city turning gold and honey-bright. The day had been perfect, almost too perfect, and Belinda's stomach was a fluttering mess of nerves and hope on the drive back to the villa.

When they arrived back at the villa, everyone scattered to their rooms in happy exhaustion, buzzing from saltwater and sunshine. Belinda lingered for a moment in the courtyard, hands pressed against her cool cheeks, willing herself to breathe. Tonight, she would see Noah. Tonight, everything might make sense. She showered slowly, letting warm water wash away the last hints of sea salt while her mind drifted to his smile, his hands, his lips. She tried on four different dresses, none quite right, before settling on a simple black one that made her feel both elegant and bold. Light makeup. The good perfume, not the mosquito-repellent lie from before.

Every few minutes she checked her phone, but still no reply. He must be busy, she told herself, cooking her birthday dinner. Something romantic. Something special. Her heart skipped like an excited teenager as she descended the stairs and followed the sound of voices and clinking cutlery to the terrace. She smoothed her dress, took one last steadying breath, and stepped into the kitchen area with a bright, nervous smile. Which immediately fell.

A stranger stood at the stove — tall, dark-haired, forearms dusted with flour, but absolutely not Noah. He glanced up, startled by her sudden appearance. 'Oh! Hi there,' he said with a friendly grin. 'You must be the birthday girl. I'm Luca.'

Belinda stared, throat suddenly dry. 'Where's Noah?'

Luca shrugged, returning to chopping herbs. 'I don't know the full story, I got a call this afternoon. Apparently, Chef had a personal emergency and needed cover. I was the lucky guy with the day off.' One by one, the happy little daydreams she had carefully built around this evening cracked apart. He hadn't replied; he hadn't come. It could mean only one thing; he didn't want to see her.

'Oh,' she breathed, forcing a smile she definitely did not feel. 'Right. That's, that's fine.' But it wasn't fine, not even close. She nodded stiffly and retreated before Luca could ask anything more, before anyone could see the disappointment burning hot behind her eyes. Noah wasn't here.

And now she knew exactly why she'd been fooling herself. He didn't feel what she felt. She was a fling he'd already regretted, and she was an absolute idiot for believing otherwise.

Chapter Thirty-Five

Dinner should have felt magical. The terrace looked like a glossy magazine spread again, with fairy lights twinkling above, lanterns glowing softly, a warm island breeze rustling the vines around the pergola. Carla had gone full Pinterest-on-espresso with silver "50" balloons, sparklers jammed into the cake, champagne chilling in buckets like they were entertaining royalty instead of one exhausted family and a guilt-ridden daughter.

Despite that, all Belinda could see was the empty space where Noah should have been standing. She smiled when she was supposed to smile, laughed when Carla delivered one of her dramatic, exaggerated stories. She blew out the candles, Carla insisted on all fifty, everyone nearly passed out helping her extinguish them. She accepted hugs, presents, and compliments. But her heart? Her heart was somewhere else entirely. Carla leaned in close while Jason and Jake debated how many shots one could safely consume before cliff-jumping became a legally questionable activity.

'He has to have a reason, Belinda,' she whispered,

squeezing her hand. 'This isn't like him. Something unexpected must've come up.' Belinda just nodded, eyes fixed on the dark villa entrance, willing Noah to walk through it, but he didn't. She checked her phone under the table. Still nothing. Annalise, sitting opposite, saw the movement, and her guilt twisted harder. She pushed peas around her plate for a full minute before glancing up, only to find her mother staring off into the distance, breathing through a pain she didn't want anyone to see.

Jake, oblivious to the emotional hurricane, clinked his glass. 'A toast! To Belinda, who does fifty better than most people do twenty-five.'

Everyone cheered, and Carla threw in a wolf-whistle. But Belinda barely tasted the champagne on her lips. Finally, Jason stood and pulled his mother up into the aisle for a dance while the portable speaker played some jazzy number he had picked earlier. Belinda swayed with him, smiling gently, because she did love her son, and she was grateful they were here, together. She wrapped her arms around his shoulders and breathed him in like a memory.

But through all the music and laughter around her, she only heard silence. Noah's silence.

Carla kept darting glances toward the path that led to the driveway, every clink or rustle making her turn with hope. After the fourth time, she groaned dramatically and tossed her napkin down. 'If that man doesn't have an excellent reason for breaking my best friend's freshly awakened heart, then I will personally make him walk the plank tomorrow,' she muttered, half-serious, half-threat. Belinda let out a soft laugh, but it was fragile, like a glass about to crack. Across the table, Annalise shrank into her chair. She had wanted to protect her parents, to try to keep her family whole. Stop something wrong from happening. But now she wasn't sure she had stopped the wrong thing from happening. She might have caused it.

As dessert plates were cleared and candles burned low, Belinda wrapped her shawl tighter around her arms and lifted her eyes once more toward the villa door. This time, she didn't pretend she wasn't hoping. But hope sat sharp and painful, like a splinter that wouldn't come out. She was fifty years old today, and she had finally learned that it didn't matter how old you were, heartbreak was a bitch.

Noah sat on the terrace steps in the dark, the only light coming from the dull amber glow spilling through his living room curtains. The night around him was quiet, that deep Maltese quiet where the sea hushes everything else. Even the cicadas seemed to hold their breath. From where he sat, he could just make out the distant rise of the hillside where the villa perched. He couldn't see the terrace itself, couldn't hear the music or laughter that might be drifting up from a birthday celebration, but he imagined it. And it hurt far more than seeing it would have.

Max lay stretched at his feet, chin on Noah's boot, giving the occasional concerned huff, the canine version of Are you going to stop brooding or should I go fetch the whisky? 'Look at them, eh?' Noah mumbled, running a hand through his hair as he stared into the dark. 'Probably all dressed up. Mike turning up like some bloody knight in shining armour.' He swallowed. Even saying the man's name felt like a punch.

He pictured Belle, not the Belle he'd kissed so recently, soft and warm and tasting faintly of citrus, but a version of her smiling at her ex-husband across a candlelit table. Maybe thanking him for surprising her. Maybe letting him put a hand on her back, the way Noah had done just yesterday. Maybe realising she wanted her old life back. Noah pressed his palms together, elbows on his knees, and let the ache settle in his chest.

He thought of Sarah then, because heartbreak would always draw her memory out of the shadows. Losing her had carved a hollow through him he'd never expected to fill. For years, he'd gone through the motions, cooking because it shut his brain off, listening to music because it was easier than talking. He'd assumed that part of him, the part capable of wanting someone, of imagining a future, had died with her.

And then Belle had walked back into his life. Barefoot in his kitchen, laughing at his stupid jokes. Letting him touch her face like it meant something. And for a fleeting, dangerous moment he'd believed he might get another chance at something real. He leaned back against the stone wall, closing his eyes as memories slipped through him, two kids racing through lemon groves, teasing each other at summer picnics, him gazing at her with adoration when he was young and too naïve to know what heartbreak even was.

'She always knew how to knock me sideways,' he muttered to the dark. Max nudged his knee, tail thumping once, a gentle I'm here. Noah let out a humorless laugh. 'Good thing one of us has sense. I must've been mad thinking she'd pick me over the father of her kids.'

The villa lights flickered faintly in the distance, or maybe he imagined that too. Maybe he imagined everything. A fantasy, a second chance that had never really existed. He scrubbed his hands over his face. 'She probably didn't even think twice about it,' he whispered. 'Birthday dinner. Her whole family. The ex-husband showing up to talk things over. Why would she?' Max shifted closer, resting his big head in his lap, offering steady warmth. Noah stroked his fur absently.

'I was stupid. That's all.' But then he remembered her eyes just that morning, the softness there, the way she looked at him like she was stepping off a cliff and hoping he'd catch her. And for the first time all night, he let himself admit the truth. 'I miss her already.'

The words drifted out on the wind, fragile as smoke. He stayed there until the night grew cool and Max nudged him toward the door, sensing they'd both had enough. But when he finally went inside, Noah turned off the lights. He didn't want to see the emptiness of his home too clearly. Not yet.

Chapter Thirty-Six

The next morning, Belinda didn't want to leave the safe, warm cocoon of her bed. She didn't want to open her eyes and let daylight remind her that the ache in her chest was real, not some foolish, wine-soaked hallucination. She lay still, listening to the quiet villa, the clatter of someone moving about downstairs, the distant sound of Jason arguing with Carla over the shared bathroom, the unmistakable thrum of someone's phone buzzing endlessly. Normal family noise. Everything felt painfully normal. Except her.

Belinda curled deeper into the sheets, hugging one pillow to her stomach like it might hold her together. She could still smell him if she tried, that faint hint of rosemary and sea salt that clung to his shirt at the cafe. The warmth of his hand sliding down her spine when he kissed her, and the look in his eyes. God, the way he'd looked at her, like she was something precious. Her throat tightened.

Maybe something happened, Carla had insisted last night, refilling her champagne glass too many times. Possibly an emergency. Maybe he's sick. Carla had seen her goddaughter's pinched expression at the table, the way Annalise had kept her head low, the way guilt clung to her like smoke and planned to have a quiet word, but at the time just wanted to support her friend in her hour of need.

Now, morning light crept along the edges of the curtains, urging Belinda up. And with it, a tiny flutter of hope whispered: Go down, maybe he's there. Maybe he'll smile at you, apologise, kiss you in that quiet, secret way he does. Eventually, that whisper pushed her out of bed. She dressed slowly, choosing soft linen shorts and a loose blouse — practical, she told herself. Comfortable. Nothing that said my heart is hanging by a thread and I'm praying you're in that kitchen. She didn't bother with makeup. She didn't want to look eager. Or desperate.

Her pulse drummed harder with each step down the staircase. By the time she reached the ground floor, she could hear someone moving around in the kitchen, pans clinking, cupboard doors opening. Familiar, comforting sounds. Her breath caught. Maybe… maybe it was him. Belinda placed a hand on the doorframe, steadied herself, and then pushed the door open.

And there was Magda. Not Noah. The older woman glanced over her shoulder, her silver bun perfectly neat as always. She was chopping fruit with her usual brisk efficiency, as if nothing at all were amiss. 'Good morning, Belinda,' Magda said warmly. 'I'm making a platter before the others descend like vultures. Coffee? You look like you need one.'

Belinda opened her mouth, a hopeful question on her tongue, but nothing came out. Noah's apron wasn't on its hook. His knives weren't on the counter. Even that damn gecko had disappeared. His absence pressed against her like a physical weight. 'Where's,' her voice failed. She swallowed and tried again. 'Where's Noah? Is he… running late?'

Magda's knife paused mid-slice. 'Ah.' A single syllable, heavy and knowing. She set the knife down gently and wiped her hands on a towel. 'He called late last night,' she said carefully. 'Told me he wouldn't be in today. Or for a while.'

Belinda's breath stuttered. 'For a while?'

Magda nodded softly. 'He didn't explain. Just asked if I could cover breakfast. Something must have happened.'

Belinda's pulse throbbed painfully in her temples. 'Oh,' she whispered, the word a small, broken thing. 'Right. Okay. I understand.' But she didn't; she didn't understand anything. All she knew, with a sudden cold clarity, was that whatever fragile, shimmering thing had begun to form between her and Noah had shattered without warning. She gripped the edge of the counter to steady herself as the last threads of hope slipped through her fingers.

Belinda pushed a piece of melon around her plate, smearing it across the porcelain rather than lifting it to her mouth. Breakfast chatter swirled around her — the scrape of chairs, Jason complaining about the strength of the coffee, Susan complimenting Carla's kaftan — but it all sounded muffled, like she was underwater.

The villa's terrace, usually her favourite place in the mornings, felt unbearably bright. Even the sea glittering below seemed to mock her. He didn't come; he didn't call; he didn't answer you — beat through her head like a drumbeat. She swallowed hard, forcing her eyes down to her untouched plate. Sophia, the ever-smiling concierge, arrived just as Carla was demanding more croissants from poor Magda. Dressed impeccably in a linen suit despite the rising heat, she carried her clipboard tucked under one arm.

'Good morning, everyone!' she chimed, her cheerfulness somehow both genuine and intrusive. 'I just wanted to make sure everything was perfect for your day.'

'Perfect except for the hangover,' Carla muttered, shielding her eyes dramatically. 'Did we really need all those bottles of champagne last night?'

'Yes,' Jason said flatly. 'Yes, you did.'

Sophia cleared her throat delicately. 'I also wanted to confirm that Chef Luca will be with you for the remainder of your stay.'

Belinda's head jerked up, and Carla blinked. 'Luca? Not Noah?'

Sophia shook her head, her brow wrinkling. 'Noah contacted management again late last night. He asked to be replaced for the duration of this booking. It was very unexpected. He's normally incredibly dependable.'

Each word felt like another crack running through Belinda's chest. 'Oh,' she managed, arranging her features into something neutral. 'Well. Thank you for letting us know.'

Sophia hesitated, genuine confusion flickering in her expression. 'If you'd like me to check with him?'

'No,' Belinda said too quickly. 'No. That won't be necessary.'

Across the table, Annalise went rigid, her fork freezing halfway to her mouth. Carla, however, narrowed her eyes like a hawk scenting trouble. Sophia gave a polite bow of her head. 'Please call me if you need anything at all. Enjoy your day.'

When she left, the terrace fell quiet until Carla slapped her hands on the table. 'Right! Enough moping.'

'Carla.'

'No.' She pointed her knife at Belinda with the authority

of a seasoned general. 'You are not sitting here all day pining over a man who can sauté feelings into his risotto. We are doing something fun.'

Jason choked on his coffee. 'Fun for whom?'

'All of us.' Carla grinned wickedly. 'Sophia told me there's a stunning ranch just outside Mdina. Horseback riding, scenic trails, gorgeous views, they even provide a luxury picnic. It's a perfect antidote'

Jason visibly paled. 'Horses? Like… big horses?'

'Most horses are big, darling,' Carla replied sweetly.

'I'm not getting on something with eyes like that,' he muttered. 'They're crazy beasts.'

Jake laughed, full-throated and delighted, although he had a thoughtful look on his face. 'Come on, man, it'll be great. I haven't ridden in years. I'd love to go.'

And just like that, Jason straightened, bravado snapping into place. 'Well, if Jake's going,' he said, trying and failing to sound nonchalant. 'I mean, yeah. Horses. Sure. Why not?'

Carla clapped her hands. 'Wonderful! It's settled.'

Annalise shifted in her seat, pushing eggs around her plate. Belinda forced a smile, though every muscle in her face trembled. 'It sounds lovely,' she said softly. 'Really.'

Carla squeezed her hand under the table. Her voice gentled. 'We're going to keep you busy today, sweetheart. No overthinking. No spiraling. Just sunshine, horses, and letting your best friend bully you into having fun.'

Belinda let out a thin, shaky breath. Behind them, Annalise bit her lip so hard it nearly bled. The guilt that had been gnawing at her since yesterday now rose like bile in her throat. She stared at her mother's sad, hopeful smile. And wondered how on earth she could ever fix what she'd broken?

Chapter Thirty-Seven

Noah balanced on the ladder, holding the newly painted blue shutter in place, trying to align the hinge with the screw hole. The salt-tinged breeze ruffled his shirt, but sweat still clung to his neck, partly from the heat, mostly from the knot of frustration pulsing in his chest. He'd deliberately shopped at the small supermarket in Nadur that morning, avoiding the Saturday market on the harbour. Avoiding Mikiel. Avoiding everything. The less chance he had of running into anyone who might mention Belle, the better.

He tightened a screw, jaw clenched. *She didn't choose you; get over it.* He didn't hear the footsteps until a familiar gravelly voice barked up at him. 'Those shutters were fine before, you know. But if you want more work for yourself, I can always bring you my boat to repaint.'

Noah jolted so hard he nearly lost his grip. 'Bloody hell, Mikiel!'

Below him stood the old fisherman, cap in hand, white beard windblown, sandals dusty from the path. He looked faintly triumphant. 'You're supposed to be at the market,'

Noah groused, coming down the ladder as if that might make Mikiel vanish.

'And you're supposed to be cooking for the holidaymakers,' Mikiel shot back. 'Carla messaged me.'

'Carla,' Noah muttered, rubbing his face. 'Of course she did.'

Mikiel's sharp old eyes scanned him. 'You're avoiding me.'

'Don't be ridiculous, of course I'm not,' Noah lied, picking up his screwdriver and pretending to inspect it like it mattered.

'You are,' Mikiel said, stepping closer. 'And you're avoiding everyone else too. Even Max looks depressed.' Max, lounging in the shade, huffed as if in agreement.

Noah sighed, defeated. 'I just needed some space. That's all.'

Mikiel folded his arms. 'From what? That woman you've been making heart eyes at for days?'

'I haven't…'

'Pah.' Mikiel waved a hand. 'I've seen kittens with more subtlety.'

Noah turned away, fixing a hinge that did not need fixing. 'It's not going to work.'

'Why not?'

'Because it isn't,' he snapped, more sharply than intended. 'Drop it, Mikiel.'

The old man studied him for a long, quiet moment. Then he walked to the terrace rail, looked out over the cliffs toward the distant villa, a white speck against the golden rock. 'You've lost too much, Noah,' he said, voice gentler now. 'And you've lived inside your grief so long you think there's no door out. But this woman, she opened one.'

Noah swallowed. 'You don't know what you're talking about.'

'I know when a man starts fixing shutters at six in the morning instead of working, he's hiding from something,' he grinned.

Noah's throat tightened. 'It's complicated.'

'Everything worth having is,' Mikiel said simply. 'Love doesn't arrive perfect. It arrives messy. Scary. Wrong timing, wrong circumstances… but still right.' He leaned on his stick. 'Some chances come once, Noah. Maybe twice if you're blessed. And you,' he poked Noah in the chest, 'are blessed more than you care to admit.'

Noah stepped back, hands on his hips, looking anywhere but the old man's face. 'I can't,' he said quietly. 'Okay? I can't.'

Mikiel nodded slowly, accepting the words though not believing them. 'If that's truly your heart speaking, then I'll leave it.' Noah exhaled. 'But if it's fear talking,' Mikiel added, eyes twinkling despite his stern tone, 'then you're being a bloody idiot.'

Noah's laugh cracked in his throat, a sound too close to breaking. Mikiel clapped his shoulder. 'Come back to the cafe when you're done playing carpenter. And bring Max. He's sick of your mood.' Max barked, tail thumping as if to say finally, someone understands me.

Noah watched the old man amble down the path, cap bobbing. The shutters gleamed a cheerful Mediterranean blue behind him, tauntingly bright. He leaned against the wall, closing his eyes. He could still feel Belle's hand in his, still taste her kiss. Noah pushed the thought away so hard it felt like something inside him cracked.

'No more,' he whispered to the empty air. But the sea

breeze, or perhaps something else, whispered back all the same.

The luxury minibus purred softly as it wound its way out of the village and toward Mdina, sunlight glinting off the gleaming white paintwork. Inside, the cool air-conditioning carried a subtle scent of citrus polish, brushing over the buttery-soft white leather seats.

Annalise and Jake had claimed the back corner, tucked together like a glossy lifestyle-magazine couple. She rested her head on his shoulder, her knees curled under her like a cat, while Jake scrolled through photos on his phone of some obscenely expensive yacht he'd once been on. Annalise laughed loudly, gazing at him with adoration written across her features.

Carla, opposite them, was animatedly recounting a story to Jason, who was doing his best to appear engaged even though he kept glancing nervously out of the window, probably imagining horses kicking, biting, bucking, or performing other horrifying activities Jason was sure were personal vendettas reserved specifically for him.

Belinda sat near the front, close enough to the driver to pretend she was enjoying the scenery, close enough to her sister for privacy but not interrogation. Susan sat beside her, hands folded neatly in her lap, her silver hair pinned back with a simple tortoiseshell clip. The morning sun caught the lines around her eyes, lines carved from years of fear, restraint, silence.

'Coffee?' Susan offered gently, holding out the little takeaway cup she'd brought with her. Belinda shook her head with a small smile.

'My stomach's too knotted.'

Susan studied her for a moment, the slight slump of her shoulders, the way she picked absently at a thread on her sundress. 'Thinking about him?'

Belinda's jaw tightened. 'I shouldn't be.'

Her sister gave a soft, understanding hum. 'You like him.'

She let out a shaky laugh. 'I do. And I hate that I do.'

The minibus curved around a bend, revealing rolling fields and distant terracotta rooftops. Belinda stared out at them, grateful for something neutral to look at. 'I don't understand what happened,' she whispered. 'One minute everything felt… possible. And the next, nothing. No message. No appearance. No, him.' She swallowed hard. 'And it hurts more than it should after such a short time.'

Susan's hand slipped over hers, warm and steady. 'It's not about time, Bee,' she said, using her childhood nickname, 'it's about connection. But… I think it was too soon. After everything.'

Blinking fast to hold back the tears, Belinda said, 'I know. I know that. It's just that, for the first time in years, I felt excited. Hopeful. Like someone actually saw me.'

Susan squeezed her hand. 'And it's wonderful you felt that. Truly. But you've been through something devastating. Your marriage ending, that's a kind of grief too. And sometimes rushing into hope, it's a way of running from the pain rather than healing it.'

Belinda closed her eyes, letting those words land. Heavy, true, unwelcome as Susan continued, her voice low and full of regret. 'I wish I'd learned it sooner myself. I stayed with Gerald for thirty-five years thinking I needed him. Thinking I wasn't me without him. I only realised I'd have been fine on my own, better, even, when it was too late to choose it.' She looked at her, eyes shining. 'I'm sorry, Bee. For everything. For disappearing, letting him stop me from seeing you. For not being there when Mom died. For letting him control every part of my life until there was hardly anything left.'

Belinda turned, her voice raw. 'You're here now. That's what matters.'

Her sister's smile trembled, but it was real. 'Yes. And I won't vanish again. I promise you that.'

From the back, Carla shouted, 'So, does anyone know if horses can smell fear? Because Jason's sweating like a nun in a nightclub.' Jason groaned, sinking lower in his seat. Annalise laughed. Jake patted him on the back with a fraternity-brother confidence.

Belinda leaned her head on Susan's shoulder, exhaustion and affection washing over her at once. 'Maybe,' she whispered, 'I do need to find myself again.'

'And you will,' she replied. 'And when you do, the right man won't vanish. He'll be waiting.'

Belinda wanted to believe that, but the ache in her chest whispered it wouldn't be Noah.

Chapter Thirty-Eight

The bedroom door stuck at first, the old wood swollen from years of sea air and disuse. Noah pressed harder, shoulder braced, until it gave with a reluctant groan that echoed down the silent hallway. The late-morning light filtered through the cracks in the ancient shutters, dust drifting lazily in the pale beams like tiny ghosts disturbed from sleep. The air held the stale, forgotten stillness of a place sealed away, a place waiting for something that never came.

He stood on the threshold, Max hovering at his heels, tail low but wagging anxiously as if sensing the significance of this moment. Noah's chest constricted. 'This is stupid,' he muttered, though nothing about this felt stupid. It felt terrifying, necessary and very long overdue. He stepped inside. The floorboards creaked under his weight, each groan of the wood a reminder of every day he'd walked past this door pretending he didn't see it. The bed was still made with crisp white sheets, extra pillows, lace-edged shams Sarah had jokingly called fancy doilies. But the romance of the room had faded. Literally.

And suddenly, Noah couldn't breathe. He crossed to the shutters, fingers trembling, and threw them open. Light burst into the room — bright, Mediterranean, unapologetically alive. It poured across the floorboards, chased the shadows from the corners, and struck the abandoned petals so they gleamed like pieces of old parchment. A warm breeze swept in with the light, bringing the scent of the sea and sun-warmed stone, stirring the curtains like a sigh. Max trotted forward and jumped onto the bed as if giving permission.

Noah leaned both palms on the windowsill and closed his eyes. He'd imagined this moment countless times, always with dread, always with guilt. As if opening the shutters, touching the sheets, letting fresh air in would somehow be a betrayal. As if moving forward meant leaving Sarah behind. But today, something felt different.

Maybe it was the ache still lodged in his chest from Belle's absence. Maybe it was hearing her laughter again, remembering how it had made something dormant inside him flicker awake. Maybe it was Mikiel's gruff wisdom: You only get one heart, ħabib. Shame to let it dry out like an old net. Maybe it was the realisation that hope hurt, but avoiding it hurt worse.

'Sarah,' he whispered into the sunlit room. 'I miss you, you know I'll always miss you.' His voice cracked raw on the last words. 'But I don't think you'd want me living like this. Like a ghost haunting my own house.' Max nudged his leg, whining softly. Noah laughed under his breath, shaky and small. 'Yeah, boy. I know.' He moved to the bed, sat heavily, and picked up a dried petal between his fingers. It crumbled instantly, dusting his palm with beige flecks. 'Maybe,' he said slowly, 'it's time.'

Not to forget, he would never do that. But to breathe

and to live again, even if Belle would not be part of it. He brushed the rest of the petals into a pile and tipped them gently into the wastebasket. Then he stripped back the sheets, opened every window, and let the Maltese sun stretch its golden arms into the room that had waited far too long for life.

The horse ranch sat just outside Mdina, all rolling fields, sunburnt fences and the faint, unmistakable aroma of horse poop, which Carla immediately declared was "very authentic" and Annalise declared was "an assault on her nasal passages." Their luxury minibus rolled to a stop in front of the stables, all white leather, tinted windows and far too much glamour for a place where manure was casually considered part of the décor. A cheerful stable hand named Marc waved them in. 'Welcome! We will find the perfect horse for each of you in no time at all, then we'll be off.'

Jason visibly paled. 'Perfect horse?' he croaked. 'As in gentle and elderly? Preferably half-asleep? Ideally stuffed?'

Jake clapped him on the back. 'Relax. I think we established horses can sense fear.' Jason stared at him in mute horror. 'That's literally the worst thing you could have said.'

Susan, who had apparently entered a serene, post-Gerald Zen phase, sighed contentedly. 'It's such a beautiful day. I feel like a cowgirl.'

Carla winked at her. 'Darling, you *look* like a cowgirl. Sexy boots and all,' and Susan flushed at the compliment. Belinda wasn't listening; she was scanning her phone for signals, for messages that weren't there. Noah's silence sat like a stone in her stomach. Still, she smiled politely as introductions were made and Marc led them down the line of horses. 'Let's start assigning mounts,' he said brightly. 'Annalise, you look confident. This is Starling.'

Starling was a glossy, elegant mare with eyelashes most

supermodels would kill for. Annalise preened, instantly smitten with her ride. 'She's perfect.' Next, he gave Jake a muscular stallion named Brutus, who immediately nuzzled him like they were old friends. *Of course he did,* thought Jason sourly. Jake had that universal charm usually reserved for Disney princesses.

Then Marc came to Carla. 'This,' he said, holding her bridle firmly, 'is Bella Donna,' as the horse pranced a little dance and tossed her mane like a diva entering a room. Carla clasped her hands dramatically. 'She knows she's fabulous, like me. I love her.'

They all laughed at that and then came Susan, who was bestowed with a small, elderly, vaguely potato-shaped horse named Turnip. 'Oh, he's precious,' she squealed, hugging him around the neck as Jason paled even further. He'd been hoping the half-asleep nag would be his, but now there were only two left. He swallowed audibly.

'Something small,' he begged. 'Something safe. Something like a broom?'

But Marc just beamed and gestured grandly. 'And this is Apocalypse.' The horse was a towering, muscle-bound bay, and with eyes that rolled back into their sockets, stomped a hoof, snorted a plume of steam, and gave Jason the side-eye of doom.

'That's not a horse,' Jason whispered. 'That's a mythological punishment.' Carla doubled over laughing at the sheer panic on his face.

'He likes strong riders,' Marc added helpfully.

'I am *not* a strong rider. I'm not even a *rider;* I'm a pedestrian with a barely used gym membership!' Apocalypse leaned forward, sniffed Jason's hair, and let out a snort so powerful it tousled his fringe. Belinda tried and failed, to smother her giggles. Even the ache in her chest lightened a little.

'Oh, honey,' she said affectionately, 'we believe in you.'

'I don't,' Jason muttered as the horse stamped, impatient to be off. 'Apocalypse definitely doesn't.'

Finally, Marc turned to Belinda, 'and for you, something calm and steady, I think. This is Lavender.' Lavender, a gentle dun mare with big soft eyes, stepped forward and nudged her shoulder sweetly. Belinda stroked her nose, grateful at least something today was gentle.

Behind her, Jason was making his will on his phone. 'If I die,' he said, climbing reluctantly into the saddle, 'tell Noah he owes me one; it's his bloody fault we're here.'

Belinda flinched at the sound of his name but pulled herself ungracefully into the saddle as Carla leapt on with practiced ease. 'God, I've missed having a beast between my thighs,' she said with a wicked grin, leaning forward to pat the horse's neck. And as they all mounted up and prepared to trot off toward the Maltese hills, Jason's panicked voice floated across the stable yard like a mantra.

'I'm gonna die, I'm gonna die, I'm gonna die.'

Chapter Thirty-Nine

The horses settled into an easy rhythm as the group followed the trail guide up a gentle slope overlooking Malta's sunlit countryside. Golden fields rippled in the warm breeze, dotted with olive trees and bursts of wildflowers. The distant dome of Mdina glowed like a pearl against the sky. Lavender carried Belinda steadily, her ears flicking back in calm reassurance. Carla's Bella Donna strutted as if she were modelling for an equestrian catalogue. Starling and Brutus kept pace ahead, Annalise's laughter carried by the wind while Jake's deep voice floated back in warm, teasing replies.

Behind them, Jason clung to Apocalypse like a backpack strapped onto a very disgruntled dragon. 'Stop looking at the birds like that,' Jason hissed. 'They didn't do anything to you. Don't start something.' Apocalypse ignored him entirely, but he flicked his tail sharply across Jason's leg, making him yelp loud enough that Susan nearly fell off Turnip from laughing. They wove through limestone paths, climbed shallow ridges, and trotted beneath a stretch of cooling pine trees. Jason eventually discovered that Apocalypse was less likely to buck him if he whispered constant positive affirmations. 'You're strong,' he murmured. 'You're majestic. You're terrifying, but in a good way.'

By midday, the trail opened onto a vast overlook above terraced fields, the sea shimmering faint blue on the horizon. A long table had already been set under a canvas canopy: chilled champagne, fresh Maltese bread, cheeses, olives, stuffed aubergines, pastizzi, fruit platters, tiny pastries dusted with sugar. Luxury picnic indeed.

'Now this,' Carla said, swinging gracefully off Bella Donna, 'is the sort of riding I approve of.'

They all dismounted, Jason with the help of two guides, gravity, and a prayer, and settled under the shade. Plates were filled, glasses clinked, and laughter rose freely. Even Belinda felt a softness return to her chest; the sun, the breeze, the peace — it eased something in her.

Jake, however, was strangely quiet. Annalise noticed first. 'Everything okay, babe?' He smiled, not his usual grin, but something brighter, steadier. He stood up, brushing grass from his jeans.

'Actually,' he said, 'there's something I've been wanting to do, and now seems like the perfect time.' Carla's fork froze halfway to her mouth, and Belinda felt her heart stutter. Jake stepped in front of Annalise and held out his hand. 'Come here, Lise.' She blinked, confused but smiling as she let him pull her up.

Then he dropped to one knee, and the world seemed to hold its breath. 'Annalise, you've made every part of my life better. You're my best friend, my partner, my favourite human. I don't want another day to pass without you knowing I'm in this forever.' He opened a small velvet box that he'd pulled from his pocket. 'Will you marry me?'

A tiny squeak escaped Annalise. Then a gasp, followed by a sob. Then, 'Yes! Yes, oh my God, yes!' She practically launched herself into his arms. The group erupted in cheers. Susan wiped her eyes. Carla filmed the entire thing, cooing dramatically. Belinda hugged them both, joy fluttering through her, genuine joy, uncomplicated, and for a moment she forgot everything else. Jason, still pale from riding, raised his glass.

'Congratulations, guys! And if Apocalypse doesn't murder me on the way back, this will officially be the best day of the trip!'

The breeze carried Annalise's delighted laughter across the hillside as Jake spun her around, her hair catching the sunlight, the island stretching endlessly and beautiful around them.

Noah closed the bedroom door gently behind him. The windows were open now, letting in the clean air. The bed was stripped; the brittle rose petals swept away; the dust banished. For the first time in years, that room didn't feel like a wound. Satisfied and wrung out in equal measure, he clipped Max's lead on and headed down the sun-warmed path toward the harbour. Max trotted beside him like a four-legged bodyguard, chest out, tail high, the proud escort of a man who had, frankly, survived some feelings.

Franko's café sat right on the water, its old wooden tables worn smooth by decades of elbows, cards, coffee cups, and arguments about football, politics and women. The Boċċi boys were already there. Mikiel sat at the centre like a wrinkled king, tiny glass of espresso in hand, flat cap tipped back on his head. The others, Frans, Turi, and Paolo were mid-argument about whether the 1978 championship had been "rigged by idiots" or merely "played by blind fools."

Mikiel spotted Noah and grinned. 'Ah! The carpenter-chef arrives! Come, sit. We are just discussing important life matters.'

'You were shouting about referees,' Noah said, dropping into a chair next to him.

'Life,' Mikiel said, shrugging with his perpetual grin. Max received immediate honorary membership via a biscuit. Noah stared out at the water while they talked nonsense around him, boats clinking against moorings, gulls arguing overhead, the air rich with coffee and salt.

Finally, Frans leaned in. 'You have the face of a man who is either sick or in love.'

'Or constipated,' Turi added helpfully.

'In love,' Mikiel corrected, squinting at Noah. 'He has already had the constipated face. This is different again.'

Noah huffed a breath through his nose. 'It's not happening.'

'Why?' Paolo asked, waving at the waiter to bring them more coffees.

'Because…' He trailed off.

Mikiel's voice dropped suddenly serious. 'You didn't say why. Why this sudden change of heart?' Noah tightened his jaw. 'Listen to me, boy,' Mikiel said, leaning closer, elbows on the table. 'We are old. We have buried friends. Wives. Dreams. We are not scared of the truth. So, you don't need to be.'

Noah looked down at his hands. 'I think she chose her old life. Her ex.'

There was a beat of silence, then all four men burst out

laughing. 'Men are so stupid,' Frans said, wiping tears of mirth from his face.

'You saw her eyes,' Mikiel said, prodding him in the chest. 'They were not the eyes of a woman going backwards.'

'You don't disappear from work and hide from markets if you don't care,' Paolo added. Mikiel had obviously been gossiping again.

Turi leaned forward. 'Love is not calm, Noah. Love is scary, ugly and confusing. If it doesn't frighten you, it's not real.'

Mikiel tapped the table hard, making the small espresso cups dance. 'You lost love once, but that wasn't your fault.' He tapped it again, gentler this time. 'But if you lose this because you didn't even try… that one will hurt forever.' Max let out a low, supportive woof. Mikiel smiled at the dog. 'Even the dog agrees.'

Silence wrapped around Noah. He thought of Belle's laugh. Her eyes. Her body pressed close to his when the world felt small and safe. Then he thought of the text she'd sent. *Wish you were here.*

Mikiel pushed his chair back. 'Finish up your coffee, then go.'

Noah blinked. 'Go?'

'To the villa,' Mikiel said simply. 'Not to demand or to accuse. Just to say what is in your heart,' he thumped his chest to emphasise his point.

'What if I'm wrong?'

Mikiel shrugged. 'Then you are a brave man who tried.' The others nodded. Max stood up, tail already wagging as if he agreed with this plan of action. Noah stood slowly, like a man stepping off a cliff with no idea if he'd land or fly. He looked back once at the old men, hesitating. Mikiel waved him away. 'Go before I throw this coffee at you.' Noah laughed, a real, surprised sound, and turned toward home, stopped and then turned toward the villa, toward Belle and the possibility of a second chance at love.

Whether it ruined him… or saved him.

Chapter Forty

The sun was sliding low over the Maltese hills when the minibus pulled back into the villa's gravel drive, tyres crunching softly. Laughter spilled out even before the doors opened, the kind of loose, giddy laughter that comes from sun, champagne and life-altering news. Annalise and Jake were still buzzing, hands laced together, showing off the ring to anyone with eyes. Carla squealed again, even though she'd already seen it at least twelve times.

'It's still breathtaking,' she declared, grabbing Annalise's hand. 'I'm crying again. I don't care.'

Jason climbed out more slowly, limping slightly. Apocalypse had not gone gently, but he was smiling, genuinely smiling. The first genuine smile Belinda had seen from him since he'd arrived. As everyone drifted toward the villa, Susan chatting animatedly with Carla about destinations for "freedom trips," Annalise dragging Jake inside to FaceTime her friends, Jason paused by the low stone wall and glanced back at his mother.

'Hey… Mom?'

Belinda, still warm from the sun and tight with conflicting emotion, turned to him. 'What's up, sweetheart?' He shoved his hands into his pockets, weight shifting from one foot to the other.

'I'm… I'm going back to New York tomorrow.'

Her heart gave the smallest jolt. 'Already?'

He nodded, jaw flexing as he ran a hand through his hair. 'Yeah. I booked a flight while we were having lunch. I… I want to try to fix things with Alicia.' Belinda studied his face, the fear there, the hope, the stubborn love that refused to die quietly.

'Even after what she did?' She asked gently, eyes full of concern.

He let out a slow, considered breath. 'Yeah. Even after that.' He looked out across the grounds, eyes dark. 'We've never really talked properly. Not about what we actually want. We just floated, kind of drifted along. Acted like everything was fine until it wasn't.'

Belinda stepped closer, resting a hand on his arm. 'I think that's where your father and I went wrong,' she said softly. 'We stopped talking. Or we talked about bills and schedules and who was picking up who. But never about how we really felt.'

Jason looked back at her. 'Do you regret it?'

She thought about Noah, his silence and about missed chances. 'Not talking?' she asked. He nodded. 'Every day,' she admitted. 'We loved each other once. But love can't survive without honesty. Without listening.' She squeezed his arm. 'If you're going to try again, don't go back pretending nothing happened. Tell her how much it hurt you. Ask her what she's really afraid of. And listen, even if you don't like the answer.'

Jason swallowed. 'And if it doesn't work?' he asked

quietly, looking like the small boy who'd always been so serious.

'Then you'll know you tried. And you won't wake up at fifty wondering where everything went wrong,' she said with a brittle laugh. He pulled her into a hug, awkward, fierce, sudden. Belinda wrapped her arms around him, holding him like she had when he was small and the world had felt simpler.

'Thanks, Mom.'

'Anytime,' she murmured into his hair.

Behind them, Carla shouted, 'We're opening the celebration champagne in case anyone has made any more life-altering decisions!' Jason pulled back, wiping his eyes as Belinda laughed, a real, warm, broken-open laugh. And for the first time that day, her heart felt a little less heavy.

The gravel crunched beneath Noah's boots as he and Max approached the villa. He almost turned back twice, once at the gate, once at the cypress tree, but something stubborn and stupid and painfully hopeful kept him moving forward. Max padded along at his side, tail swinging like a metronome for courage. He was halfway up the drive when the front door opened and he saw a man stepping inside.

Tall, broad-shouldered and immaculate in his suit. If Noah hadn't tortured himself the night before by Googling Mike McGuire and Belinda McGuire, scrolling through years of glossy photos of them smiling at galas, hands at the small of each other's backs, sunlit yachts and champagne flutes, he still would've known. It was him. There was no mistaking that kind of polish, that kind of life. The man paused just long enough in the doorway to look back, adjust his cuffs, and smile at someone inside before the door closed softly behind him.

And just like that, Noah's chest collapsed. Max let out a low, uncertain whine, glancing between Noah and the now-innocent-looking front door. 'I shouldn't have come,' Noah whispered to himself. In his mind, the pictures replayed. Belle in satin gowns, leaning into that same man and laughing. Belle in oversized sunglasses on yachts far fancier than the tiny fishing boat where she'd kissed Noah like she meant it. Her hand resting easily on that man's arm, familiar, comfortable, history-rich and life-rich.

All the things Noah was not. He felt ridiculously out of place suddenly, with salt on his skin, old trainers, the faint smell of paint and sea air still clinging to him. A man who sanded shutters and panicked around feelings. A man who had fallen for a woman with a life that didn't have room for him. Max pressed closer, sensing the shift, ears flat, tail slowing. Noah shoved his hands into his pockets to stop them from shaking. Of course he'd come. Of course, he'd convinced himself the wise old men were right, that love was something you fought for.

And of course… he'd waited too long. He stared at the front door, willing it to open again, not so he could go in, but so he could confirm what he already knew. She's chosen him. Max nudged his thigh, soft and insistent. 'I know, I know,' Noah murmured. 'Come on, let's go.'

But his feet wouldn't move; somewhere inside, laughter echoed faintly. Glasses clinked and footsteps crossed polished stone floors. A life that wasn't his, and a woman who was never really his.

Chapter Forty-One

The villa lounge was buzzing in that loose, end-of-day way, shoes kicked off, hair messy from sun and wind, champagne already half poured "just in case." Carla burst in, clutching her phone as if it contained state secrets. 'You are all going to die of jealousy,' she announced dramatically, sinking onto the sofa. 'The captain texted me.'

Belinda, seated by the window, looked up. 'The handsome captain?'

'The very one,' Carla beamed, thrusting the screen toward her. 'He's invited me to dinner tonight. Real dinner, not boat sandwiches. Proper food, linen napkins, probably candles.'

Belinda felt something warm loosen in her chest as she looked at her. 'You should go.'

Carla blinked rapidly. 'I was going to go, anyway. Not only is he gorgeous, he's smart too; he speaks several languages.'

'No,' Belinda said gently. 'I mean really go. Don't worry

about me. Don't stay in because you think I'll fall apart. It's about time you looked at another man.'

Carla's teasing expression softened. 'Are you sure?'

Belinda smiled, a real one this time. 'I am.'

There was a knock at the front door, and Jake went to answer it. When he stepped back into the lounge, his usual confident posture was replaced with something tense. Behind him stood Mike. Silence fell like a dropped glass. Carla was on her feet in seconds. 'What the hell is he doing here?'

Mike lifted both hands calmly. 'I came to apologise.' Belinda didn't move. 'To you and, more importantly, to Belinda,' he continued, glancing directly at Carla, oddly sincere. 'I shouldn't have shown up like that and I shouldn't have made assumptions. I spoiled her birthday, and I'm sorry.'

Carla folded her arms, lips tight. 'You did.' She paused and then added, 'fine, apology noted. Not forgiven. But noted.' She stepped aside enough to let him further in, but only just.

Jake cleared his throat, trying to lighten the atmosphere. 'While we're all here together, I should probably mention something happy.'

Mike raised an eyebrow. 'Oh?'

Jake smiled and wrapped an arm around Annalise's shoulders as she appeared in the doorway. 'We're engaged.' There was a split second of silence.

'You're joking,' Mike breathed, a smile lighting up his face.

'Deadly serious,' Carla said, already reaching for champagne.

Belinda felt a swell of pride as she hugged her daughter

tightly as Mike let out a low laugh of shock. 'Well, that sure is something happy. Congratulations, sweetheart.'

Belinda stepped forward, calm, composed. 'And since we're on the topic of happy events,' she said coolly, turning back to him, 'the next time I expect to see you is at that wedding.' The implication hung heavy in the air — no more voice messages as he panicked about the new life he was starting, no more surprise visits or convincing the kids they might get back together.

Mike nodded slowly. 'Understood.'

Carla lifted her glass. 'Right. If awkward emotional confrontations are done, I'd like to officially toast to champagne, engagements, and my sex life restarting.'

Belinda laughed, and for the first time in days, it didn't hurt. Somewhere inside her, a quiet certainty began to grow. She wasn't looking backwards. Not anymore; from now on she was only going to look forward.

Noah found Mikiel at the harbour, half inside the belly of his fishing boat, muttering violently at a very stubborn net. The Santa Marija bobbed gently against the quay, her paint chipped, her ropes coiled with the lazy familiarity of a life lived at sea. Mikiel's old radio crackled in the background, spitting out a tinny Maltese folk song. Noah hopped down onto the deck. Max did not hop, just waited to be lifted onboard like the small prince he was.

'You're avoiding me again,' Mikiel said without looking up.

'I'm not, I'm here, aren't I?' Noah replied, settling Max safely on deck.

'You are,' Mikiel said, tying off with sharp, practiced fingers. Then he straightened and finally looked at him, squinting against the sun. 'Your eyes look wrong. What's going on?'

Noah leaned against a crate of bait and forced a long breath through his nose. 'I'm going to Gozo.'

Mikiel blinked twice, then joked, 'for what? You get seasick on anything bigger than a bathtub.'

'I've accepted the offer at Il-Porto Blu.' The words landed heavily. 'Fine dining for the rest of the season. It's good money, and they offer staff accommodation. Max is allowed.'

Mikiel simply stared at him for a while, then snapped, 'You are an idiot.'

Noah snorted. 'I knew that was coming.'

'You turn down that job for years,' Mikiel went on, jabbing a finger into his chest, 'and now? Now you run away and take it?'

'I'm not running,' Noah said quickly, his eyes not meeting Mikiel's. 'I'm just changing the view.'

'Ah. Running with prettier scenery.'

Noah looked out over the harbour, the sinking sun hit the water just right, turning it to broken glass of silver. 'I need to get away for a while,' he said more quietly. 'Everywhere I go here,' he paused, trying to find the words. 'A change of scenery will help, that's all.'

'She will not be fixed by distance,' Mikiel said gently, a knowing smile causing his face to wrinkle up further.

Noah smiled back, but without humour. 'I'm not trying to fix anything. Just… survive it.' A gull cried mournfully overhead, swooping across the sky. A rope creaked as the boat shifted with the tide beneath their feet. Mikiel sighed deeply and sat on an upturned bucket, suddenly looking a hundred years old.

'You always think you must solve things alone,' he said sadly. 'You think pain is a thing you can outwork.'

Noah shrugged. 'It's all I know how to do.'

Mikiel reached out with both hands and grabbed Max's face, rubbing it like it was dough. 'This one will miss me,' he told Noah. 'But he will enjoy the fresh smells.' Max licked him enthusiastically, enjoying the attention. 'You'll hate the tourists,' Mikiel continued. 'The fancy plates. The small food that costs too much.'

'I already hate the tourists,' Noah said. 'I might as well hate them somewhere new with more money.'

They stood in silence for a moment longer, then finally, Mikiel pulled him into a rough, one-armed hug. 'Go,' he said gruffly. 'Find some peace.' He stepped back, eyes sharp again. 'But remember, running and healing are not the same thing.'

Noah nodded, thankful for his old friend. 'I know.'

As he lifted Max back up and stepped off the boat, Mikiel called after him. 'If that woman ever comes asking where you are,' Noah paused, mid-step. 'I will tell her you are not lost.' Mikiel's voice softened, 'only finding your way.'

Noah didn't look back, but he felt every word.

Chapter Forty-Two

Carla stood in front of the tall mirror in her bedroom, turning slightly from side to side as she examined herself. She wore a floaty blue dress that skimmed her knees, brought out the colour of her eyes and showed just enough shoulder to feel daringly alive. Her hair, usually thrown up carelessly, had been coaxed into soft, bouncy waves. Pale peach lipstick had been applied, blotted, applied again. She let out a shaky breath. 'Get a grip,' she muttered to the reflection. 'It's just dinner with a dangerously handsome boatman. You've survived countless falls from horses, menopause and a funeral.'

Still… five years. It had been five years since the last time she'd put perfume on *for someone.* She adjusted the silver necklace at her throat, fingers trembling slightly. Behind her, Annalise hovered in the doorway. Carla saw her in the mirror before she heard her. 'You're going to burn a hole in the carpet if you keep fidgeting like that,' Carla said lightly. 'Come in, darling.'

Annalise stepped inside, her eyes darting nervously around the room. 'I just wanted to see how you were.'

Carla raised one knowing brow. 'And not because you're about to explode from keeping a secret?'

Annalise flinched. Carla turned slowly, studying the younger woman, the tight shoulders, the overbright eyes. 'I've known you since you were born,' Carla said gently. 'You have the exact same guilty face you had when you cut your own fringe at six.' She paused for a beat. Then, softer, 'I'm still very thrilled for you.'

That caught Annalise off guard. 'For…?'

'For getting engaged, of course,' Carla smiled. 'Genuinely. It's wonderful to see you so happy. But doesn't your mum deserve that happiness too?'

Annalise's mouth opened, then closed with a snap. Her eyes filled faster than she'd expected. 'I didn't,' she stopped, then tried again. 'I didn't mean for anyone to get hurt.'

Carla's expression gentled immediately. She walked over and sat on the edge of the bed. 'Talk to me.'

Annalise twisted her fingers together, another childhood trait when she was nervous. 'I followed Noah into the kitchen yesterday morning.'

Carla's eyes narrowed. 'You little spy.'

'I told him,' she swallowed hard. 'I told him Mom and Dad had been talking about getting back together.' Carla went absolutely still.

'And?' she said very calmly, despite the anxiety growing inside her.

'And I told him Dad was coming on the yacht. That it was a surprise to keep talking about… fixing things.'

Silence fell. Carla sat back slowly, staring at Annalise as if she'd just confessed to stealing the Mona Lisa.

'Sweetheart,' she said, standing up. 'You didn't just stir

the pot. You took the pot, put it on a bonfire, and then threw dynamite in it.'

Annalise's chin wobbled, and tears streamed down her cheeks. 'I thought I was protecting her.'

Carla stepped forward, placing her hands gently on Annalise's shoulders. 'I know you did.' There was a long pause as she gazed at her goddaughter. 'But you hurt them both.'

Annalise's lip trembled. 'He hasn't been back. I think he thought it was true.'

She sighed slowly, running a hand over her hair. 'Well. This explains quite a lot.' She squeezed Annalise's shoulders once, grounding herself as much as the younger woman. Her voice softened, but her eyes were already sharpening with purpose. 'We have to tell your mom. *Now.* Where is she?'

Annalise swallowed. 'She and Jason went for a walk along the coast. They wanted some time to talk before he leaves tomorrow.' Carla's stomach tightened. Of course, one last quiet mother–son moment. And of course, she'd chosen this exact window of time to have the emotional equivalent of a small nuclear incident dropped on her. She crossed the room in three quick strides and rummaged through her bag, fingers closing around her phone. She hit Belinda's speed dial without hesitation.

It rang … And rang … And then, faintly; it echoed from downstairs. Carla froze. She lowered the phone slowly, staring at it. 'Damn,' she muttered. 'She must have left it behind.' She checked the time. It was far too late in the afternoon; there was far too much coastline. Too many possible walking routes. Her mind kicked into survival mode, and she dialled Mikiel, but it went straight to voicemail. Of course. She exhaled sharply through her nose and stabbed at the phone again, as if insulting it might make it work. 'For God's sake, why do people bother having a phone if they refuse to actually use it?'

Annalise hovered near the door, twisting her engagement ring nervously. 'What do we do?'

Carla straightened so fast it was almost military. 'Right.' She pointed directly at Annalise as if she were assigning a mission in a war film. 'You go and find your mom; tell Auntie Susan to stay here in case she comes back.'

Annalise blinked. 'What are *you* going to do?'

Carla grabbed her sunglasses, slid them onto her head, and reached for her clutch like a woman about to go into battle, or at least flirt very strategically. 'I am going to meet the dashing Captain Anton,' she announced, striding toward the door, 'and convince him to help me track down Mikiel.' She paused in the doorway and turned back. 'He'll know where to find Noah. And those two idiots need the truth before they ruin their own happiness permanently.'

Annalise nodded, nerves and determination battling on her face. 'I'll find her,' she said.

Carla gave her a final, approving nod. 'Good girl.'

And with that, they burst into motion, one toward the wild, winding footpaths, the other toward the sea, a handsome captain, and the beginning of a rescue mission fueled by truth, guilt, and more than a little romantic chaos.

Chapter Forty-Three

Noah stopped just inside the iron gates, the familiar hush of the graveyard settling over him like a blanket. The air smelled of sun-warmed stone and faintly sweet flowers. The cicadas were softer here, as if even they knew to show some respect. Gravel crunched under his boots as he walked the path he could have found with his eyes shut. Sarah's headstone caught the light; her name looked the same as it always had. He crouched and rested his forearms on his knees in front of it, fingers twisting together. 'Hi, love,' he whispered. 'It's me.' The words felt strange after all this time.

'I've cleaned the room,' he admitted with a breath of soft, humourless air. 'Finally, I opened the shutters. You'd like that, you always said the light was too pretty in that house to be shut out.' He picked at a loose blade of grass, rolling it between his fingers. 'I'm not running away,' he said, more to himself than to the stone. 'I just think I need to see different water for a while. Different sky.' He paused, looking up at the endless blue horizon.

'I got offered that job again, the one in Gozo. The fancy place.' He huffed. 'You'd laugh at me in a chef's jacket so clean I'd be afraid to breathe.' He swallowed, voice quieter now. 'I wanted to tell you before I go. I don't like the idea of disappearing without saying anything.' Silence pressed in around him, but it wasn't the suffocating kind. It felt calm.

'You don't have to worry about me,' he added. 'I'm still me, and I'm not forgetting you. I don't think I ever could.' He stood slowly, resting a hand briefly against the cool stone. 'Goodbye, Sarah,' he murmured. 'Just for a while.'

Back at home, he moved through the small house with surprising calm as he packed. He didn't need to take much. A few changes of clothes, the battered cookbook that had belonged to his grandmother and his knife roll, carefully wrapped. He added a spare pair of boots and the photograph of Mikiel, him, and Max looking ridiculous after a stormy fishing trip. Max followed him everywhere, tail sweeping low against the floor, suspicious of the unusual activity and the suitcases.

'No, not that,' Noah murmured when the dog tried to add a chewed tennis ball to the suitcase. 'Take the good toys.' Max's bed was folded carefully and tucked into the second case. Then the rope toy and his favourite soft, slightly mangled plush octopus. Finally, his blanket that smelled like home, paws, and loyalty. 'Can't have you slumming it,' Noah said softly.

Outside, the taxi he'd ordered pulled up, tyres crunching softly on gravel. The driver leaned out. 'You're going to the ferry port?' he asked. Noah nodded, lifting the cases into the boot. Max hopped into the back seat without being asked, nose immediately pressed to the window like a professional traveller. As the car rolled downhill toward the port, Noah looked out at the familiar stone walls, the olive trees, the slivers of blue sea between buildings. He didn't look back when his house disappeared from view.

A little while later, the ferry loomed ahead, white, hulking, waiting. The shouts of the crewmen could be heard over the hubbub of passengers waiting to board. Noah paid the driver, pulled his cases from the boot and stood in line with Max at his heels, ready to see what came next.

Carla arrived at the harbour jetty looking like a woman ready to be adored. The blue, slightly daring dress, her hair perfect and lipstick that meant business. Captain Anton was already waiting, and he was even more incredibly handsome than she remembered. He leaned casually against a railing; arms folded in a crisp white shirt that had no right fitting him that well. 'Buona sera, Bellissima,' he said, taking in her outfit with a slow, approving glance. 'I have made a reservation somewhere with candlelight and wine that costs more than my boat.'

Carla gulped but smiled brightly. 'Change of plans.'

He blinked in surprise. 'I'm sorry?'

'We are going on a mission,' she announced, grabbing his forearm urgently. 'It's a romantic emergency. There's a fisherman involved and two, possibly emotionally stunted, star-crossed lovers. Time is against us.'

Anton stared at her for a full three seconds, and then he grinned. 'I like this date already.' He gestured dramatically to the only available mode of transport, a large motorbike. Carla squinted at it.

'Where is the sidecar? Or the staff? Or the dignity?'

'I have only this,' Anton shrugged. 'You will have to

improvise.' She stared at the bike, then at her dress and then down at her heels.

'Right,' she said through gritted teeth. 'Help me.'

Anton tried very hard to be a gentleman while lifting her onto the back. Carla, meanwhile, tried very hard not to flash most of Valletta. She scrambled inelegantly into place, dress caught awkwardly around her thighs, heels dangling dangerously. 'Hold on to me,' Anton said.

'Don't get ideas,' she warned, then immediately clung to him like a koala on its eucalyptus tree in a cyclone. They tore off down the coast road, wind whipping Carla's hair into something that could only be described as "heroically tragic." By the time they skidded to a halt outside Franko's café, she had lost a shoe and most of her dignity. The old men sitting there enjoying their evening Lumincetta all looked up at their noisy arrival. Mikiel wasn't there, but Frans, Paolo and Turi were. They all blinked at the sight of Carla perched sideways on a motorbike, gripping the confused sailor like a life raft.

'Where's Mikiel?' demanded Carla, climbing down awkwardly, trying to pull down her dress and limping slightly.

Paolo sipped his drink. 'Harbour.'

Turi nodded sagely. 'Boat.'

Frans added helpfully, 'the one that is always leaking.'

Carla grabbed Anton again. 'You heard them, captain.'

Anton laughed, kicked the engine back to life. 'Round two.' She scrambled back on, legs flailing, and her remaining heel snapped clean off. Carla stared at it on the ground. 'Leave it,' Anton said. 'We have love to save.'

The bike roared away again, carrying one determined woman, one handsome captain, and one increasingly unlikely rescue plan toward the docks while the old men at Franko's shook their heads in admiration.

'Strong woman, that one,' Paolo said, still sipping his Lumincetta.

'Terrifying,' Turi agreed.

'And the sailor?' Frans added.

'Lucky man,' they said in unison.

Chapter Forty-Four

Annalise found them just as the sun was turning the cliffs gold. Belinda and Jason were sitting on a low stone wall overlooking the sea, their shoulders almost touching, talking quietly, the way people do when they don't want to scare something fragile. Annalise came to a sudden stop, chest heaving, hands braced on her knees. 'Mom.'

Belinda turned, surprised. 'Honey? What's wrong?'

Jason stood up immediately. 'Did someone fall? Is the world ending? Or is Carla having a meltdown?'

Annalise let out a breathless, hysterical laugh that sounded too close to tears. 'No. Yes. Maybe.'

Belinda was already on her feet. 'Annalise.'

Her daughter walked closer shakily, face blotchy, eyes red. 'I need to tell you something. Something awful. And I am really, really sorry.'

Belinda's stomach tightened. 'Okay,' she said gently. 'Tell me.'

Annalise twisted her fingers together. 'Yesterday morning… I followed Noah into the kitchen.'

Jason's brows furrowed. 'Why?'

'I thought,' she swallowed. 'I thought he was just a holiday thing. And I thought you were vulnerable.' Belinda felt the world sharpen around her. 'I told him,' Annalise said quickly, words tumbling over one another, 'that you and Dad had been talking about getting back together.'

Silence hit. Jason froze, staring at his sister in shock. 'Keep going,' Belinda whispered.

'I told him Dad was flying in. That he was going to surprise you. That you were going to fix things.'

Belinda's breath caught hard in her chest. Then she started laughing. It startled all of them — a broken, shaking sound that came with sudden, hot tears. 'That explains it,' she said softly.

Jason stared at her in amazement. 'Explains what?'

'Why he disappeared,' Belinda said simply. 'Why he stopped answering me.' Something inside her didn't break; it lifted. Relief. Real, vivid relief. 'He thought I lied to him,' she realised. 'He thought I chose your father.'

Annalise scrubbed away her tears. 'You're not angry?'

Belinda stepped forward and wrapped her in a hug before she could finish the question. 'I'm pretty sure you were trying to protect me.'

'I made everything worse.'

'Yes,' Belinda admitted, pulling back enough to cup her daughter's cheek. 'But now we can fix it.' She turned immediately to Jason. 'We have to find him.'

Jason blinked. 'Now?'

'Yes,' she said, already pulling him into motion. 'Now.'

Annalise hurried to keep up. 'Carla knows,' she said between breaths. 'She went to find Mikiel; she said he would know where he is.'

Jason's eyes widened. 'Is Carla not on her date?'

'She is kind of,' Annalise winced. 'With the incredibly handsome captain.'

Belinda sighed, then smiled, because of course Carla would abandon romance for her emotional crisis. 'Let's head back towards town,' Belinda declared.

Jason cracked his knuckles. 'I'm emotionally unprepared for all this, but I'm coming.'

As they started down the path toward the road, Belinda felt something almost strange. It was hope. Real, tangible, terrifying hope. Noah hadn't walked away because he hadn't cared; he'd walked away because he'd loved her enough to think she'd chosen something else.

And now she was going to find him. Before it was too late.

The ferry deck smelled of salt, diesel, and sun-warmed metal. Noah followed the painted line along the floor, Max trotting faithfully at his heel, leash loose but trust steady. The crew took his two battered suitcases without comment, they'd seen hundreds like them, people leaving, people arriving, people trying to convince themselves of something. He tipped his head in thanks and moved out onto the open deck. The sea stretched ahead, wide and glittering, sliding gently under the bow. Gozo waited somewhere beyond the haze.

Max flopped down beside his boots with a soft huff, already settling in like this was just another ordinary adventure. Noah sank onto a metal bench and wrapped his hands around the cold rail and told himself not to think about her but failed immediately.

He remembered the way she'd looked the first morning, that ridiculous skimpy short and vest set that she'd had to borrow from Carla. The way she'd laughed when he burned the toast and the way her fingers had fidgeted with the ramekin at lunch because she never quite said what she wanted, only what she thought she should want. And the kisses. God, the kisses. He squeezed his eyes shut. *You should have fought.* The thought slid in like a traitor. *You should have gone back to the villa. You should have asked. You should have told her how you felt instead of disappearing.* His fingers tightened on the rail.

Then he thought of the photographs he'd seen, glossy, perfect, unattainable. Belle in silk dresses. Belle beside a man who looked like he belonged on yachts and in champagne adverts. And then he pictured himself, paint under his nails, dog hair on his jumper, heart patched together with stubbornness and grief. 'She deserves more,' he murmured. Max nudged his knee; brow creased like he disagreed. Noah huffed out a breath and scratched behind his ears. 'Not that I don't,' he added quietly. 'But I don't want to drag her into my mess.'

The ferry engines weren't running yet, the boat rocked only slightly as passengers continued boarding. People stepped around him, families dragging wheeled suitcases, a pair of backpackers arguing over a map, a woman trying to stop a toddler from licking the rail. Life moved forward while he sat very still.

Then the ferry horn gave a short, warning blast, the final calls for boarding. Footsteps hurried, bags thumped and voices rose as people panicked about missing the boat. He felt the pull toward the rail, the pull to stand, to look back toward the city, toward the villa that held too many memories now. But he stayed seated, because if he stood, he might run straight back to her and he'd worked too hard to drag himself away.

Chapter Forty-Five

The motorbike screeched into the harbour in a swirl of dust and sea breeze, Carla clinging to Anton's waist with one hand and clutching her handbag with the other. When he finally braked, she slid off the bike with all the grace of a newborn foal, wobbling as she pulled down her dress to a respectable level.

'I'm, never, ever,' she panted, 'doing that again in a dress.'

Anton just grinned. They spotted Mikiel immediately. The old fisherman was half-buried inside the engine hatch of his boat, muttering to himself in Maltese and smelling strongly of diesel and yesterday's catch. He popped his head up when he heard Carla's voice. 'Mikiel!' she called, breathless. 'We need you!'

'That much is obvious,' he said, eyeing her wind-tangled hair and frantic expression. 'What's the emergency now?'

'It's Noah,' Carla blurted, waving her hands as if trying to summon the right words from thin air. 'We need to find him now. It's life-or-death emotional stuff. He's got the wrong idea about Belinda, and he's disappeared instead of talking to her and…'

Mikiel held up a hand. 'The stupid boy is on the ferry.'

Carla froze. 'What?'

'The Gozo ferry,' Mikiel repeated calmly. 'It's boarding now and leaves any moment.'

Carla's stomach dropped. 'Oh God. Oh no, no, no.' Her phone buzzed in her hand. She snatched it up. 'It's Annalise,' she hissed. 'Thank heavens.' She answered.

'Carla! I found Mom,' Annalise rushed. 'We're at the top of the hill. Where are you?'

'At the harbour. Mikiel says Noah's getting on a ferry right now.'

'What? We need to catch him!'

'We're on it,' Carla promised, ending the call and wondering how on earth they would get there in time. Before she could panic further, Anton was already pulling out his phone. 'What are you doing?' she asked.

'Delaying a ferry,' he said casually, as if ordering a pizza. 'I know someone on duty tonight.' Carla watched, stunned and swooning more than just a little, as he spoke in rapid Maltese, his brow furrowing in concentration. He ended the call with a nod. 'They'll stall for a few minutes,' he said. 'But not long.'

Mikiel clapped his hands together. 'Right. You two come with me.' He led them across the harbour to his ancient Morris Minor pickup, painted in once-bright turquoise but now mostly rust. The back was filled with nets, ropes, and an unmistakable eau de haddock.

Carla recoiled. 'Absolutely not. I cannot arrive at a grand romantic rescue mission smelling like fish.'

'You want to catch Noah or not?' Mikiel asked, already climbing into the driver's seat.

Carla groaned. 'Fine. But if I get scales on my dress, I'm suing someone.'

Anton chuckled and helped her into the passenger seat, which smelled even worse. Mikiel revved the engine, which wheezed like an asthmatic accordion. 'Hold tight,' he warned. 'We'll pick up your lot, then straight to the port. That ferry won't wait forever.'

Carla braced herself, muttering, 'Heels, hair, fish fumes, Belinda owes me *so* much gin for this.' And with a violent jerk, the fish-scented pickup lurched forward, setting off on its heroic, chaotic rescue mission.

Noah stood at the rail of the ferry, Max leaning heavily against his leg, tail thumping uncertainly. The sun hung low, painting the water in molten gold, and normally Noah would have appreciated the view and the soft slap of waves against the hull, the quiet murmur of passengers settling in. But today it only made him more wound up. He checked his watch for the third time in five minutes; the ferry should have left already. 'What's the holdup?' he muttered.

Max whined softly, nuzzling Noah's hand. 'I know, boy. I know. We just need patience.' Rubbing the dog's ears, he tried to ignore the restless flutter in his gut. He'd made his decision, and he was leaving. He was doing the right thing. So why wasn't the damn boat *moving*? Around him, families were still settling in trickling groups, chattering and laughing, completely unaware that every extra second was a hammer tapping at Noah's resolve.

A young deckhand in a fluorescent vest walked by, and Noah stopped him. 'Excuse me, why is there a delay?'

The man shrugged, unconcerned. 'Technical thing. Or something with the loading, I'm not sure. We'll be off soon.'

'Soon,' Noah repeated. 'Right.' The deckhand jogged off. Noah pushed a hand through his hair. He was dangerously close to overthinking, which was the last thing he needed. The longer he stayed on this deck, the easier it became for memories to seep back in. Belle laughing on the boat, her head on his shoulder. Belle's hand brushing his in the kitchen, warm and sure.

The message she sent — *wish you were here* — played over in his mind like a song that couldn't be unheard. He clenched the rail to try to ground himself. 'Stop it,' he told himself firmly. 'She's fine. She's with her family. With her ex-husband coming back. She doesn't need…' But the sentence caught halfway out of his throat, as if something deeper inside him refused to let him finish it. Max nudged him harder, sensing his turmoil. Noah let out a strangled laugh. 'You're not helping. You know that, right?'

The ferry horn sounded, not the deep blast of departure, but a shorter, almost hesitant call. Noah frowned. 'What the hell is going on?' He looked toward the ramp. More people were boarding, weird this close to departure. His determination, already hanging by a thread, frayed further with every passing minute. 'Why doesn't it just *go*?' he whispered, gripping Max's fur as if anchoring himself. 'Please just go.' But the ferry stayed stubbornly still, as though fate, or something just as maddening, had its foot on the brake, buying time he didn't want.

Or time he desperately needed.

Chapter Forty-Six

Mikiel's ancient Morris Minor pickup rattled down the coastal road like a tin can possessed, its suspension bouncing so violently that Belinda briefly wondered if they'd arrive at the ferry port in pieces, emotionally *and* physically. The smell hit her first when she climbed in. A pungent, unmistakable aroma of fish, and not the fresh market kind. The kind that had lived an entire separate life in the back of this truck.

Now she, her adult children, and the faint remnants of her dignity were trapped inside it as Mikiel accelerated with gleeful abandon. Jason clung to the metal frame behind the cab. 'Is this thing even legal?'

'No,' Annalise squeaked, grabbing onto her brother's arm as the truck lurched around a bend. 'It's definitely not legal.'

Belinda clutched the side panel, knuckles white, hair whipping around her face. 'Hold on! And don't lean out; the door latch looks like it's from 1952!'

'It *is* from 1952!' Mikiel shouted proudly over the roar

of the engine. 'Very good year for Maltese pickups!' Another bump. All three of them bounced a good three inches off the seat.

Jason groaned. 'We're not going to get to the ferry. We're going to be *jostled to death.*' But despite the chaos, the wind, the speed, the smell, Jason's steady stream of curses, Belinda felt something warm start to rise in her chest. Hope. Real, terrifying, trembling hope.

'He didn't leave because he stopped caring,' Annalise whispered beside her, eyes shining with guilt. 'He left because of me.'

Belinda squeezed her hand hard. 'We'll fix it. We will.' She tried to believe it, and the fluttering fear inside her was almost unbearable. What if she was too late? What if he'd already decided she was a complication he didn't need? The truck screeched around another bend, sending all three of them sliding toward one side like socks in a washing machine.

'Almost there!' Mikiel crowed, obviously enjoying the drama.

'Praise every saint this island has,' Jason muttered. The port finally came into view, and they all rose slightly in their seats to see that the ferry was still docked. 'IT'S STILL THERE!' Annalise shouted, relief washing over her.

Belinda's heart leapt into her throat. 'Oh, thank God.'

Mikiel slammed on the brakes. The truck fishtailed wildly before skidding to a halt with a metallic shriek that definitely wasn't part of its original design. Belinda, Jason and Annalise tumbled out of the back in a heap of limbs and relief. Carla and Captain Anton spilled out of the front of the truck. 'We made it!' she cried, waving at the boat. 'And it's still here! It's still bloody here!' She turned to Anton and, without thinking, grabbed the front of his shirt and planted a grateful, exuberant kiss on him.

Anton blinked in pleasant surprise. 'Ah. For delaying the ferry?'

'And for not letting me die on a motorbike!' Carla added.

Jason whispered to Annalise, 'Do you think that was her first kiss in years?'

'Shhh,' Annalise hissed, 'but probably.'

Belinda's chest swelled, tangled with dread and desperation and that fragile shard of hope. 'No time,' she said breathlessly as the horn sounded with a definitive call. 'Where do I go? How do I get to him?'

Carla grabbed her hand. 'Straight up the ramp, sweetheart. Before fate changes its mind.' Belinda nodded, her pulse thrumming in her ears. There was no turning back now. The ramp vibrated under Belinda's feet as she sprinted up it, her breath catching, her heart pounding so hard it sounded like a kettledrum. The only thing her mind could form was his name. *Noah. Noah. Noah.*

On the upper deck, Noah sat rigidly on a bench with Max at his feet, staring out toward the open water as if he could will the ferry to leave finally. His jaw was tight, his shoulders tense, all determination and heartbreak and exhaustion. Max's head suddenly lifted. His tail thumped once, then twice. Then the dog whipped around, ears pricked, nose twitching madly. Noah frowned. 'What is it, boy?' Max gave a soft, excited whine, the kind that meant *someone important.* And then Noah heard it. 'Noah!'

The voice hit him like a wave. He stood too quickly, heart stumbling in his chest. Belle was there, breathless, flushed, her hair wild from wind and Mikiel's death-trap truck, eyes shining with something that looked far too much like hope. He honestly thought for a moment that he had hallucinated her. 'Belle?' he breathed.

She nodded, swallowing hard. 'Yes.' She took a shaky breath. 'I have to explain something. And you need to know it before this ferry moves.' Max bounded toward her, wriggling happily. She dropped to her knees to embrace him, pressing her face into his fur before rising again. And then she told him. All of it. What Annalise had said. Why. How. The misunderstanding that had cracked everything wide open. How she'd been terrified, hurt, but still hoping he'd walk back into the villa kitchen. How she thought she'd lost him. How she'd raced here the moment she knew the truth.

When she finished, her voice trembled. 'Noah, I didn't want Mike back. I never have. That part of my life is over. What I wanted,' she hesitated. 'What I wanted was you.'

Noah inhaled sharply. He felt the relief hit like a physical blow, knees loose, chest collapsing, something unclenching so deeply he hadn't even known it was tight. 'I thought you'd gone back to your old life,' he said, his voice low, raw. 'That I'd imagined everything.'

'You didn't imagine anything.' She stepped closer. 'Not for one moment.'

For a breath, they simply stared, years of childhood memories in their eyes, longing crackling between them, and fresh hope weaving shyly through the air. He let out a shaky laugh. 'So where does that leave us?'

Belinda smiled, soft and a little teasing. 'Well, I'm not sure I'm ready for something complicated. Life's a bit messy right now.'

He nodded. 'I get that.'

'But,' she lifted her chin. 'I am very open to being good friends.'

He raised an eyebrow. 'Good friends?'

'Who kiss occasionally,' she added lightly.

His mouth curved slowly, beautifully. 'Occasionally?'

'Maybe more than occasionally,' she murmured.

Max barked once, loudly, as if giving his approval. And then Noah closed the distance. The kiss wasn't rushed or desperate. It was warm, grateful, full of rediscovered possibility. Belle's hands slid up to his shoulders; his cupped her face gently, as if she were something precious.

Somewhere behind them, a horn sounded, and the ferry shuddered as the engines rumbled to life. But neither of them noticed. They were too busy rediscovering each other. Too busy kissing, breathless and smiling and utterly, hopelessly relieved.

Too busy feeling the world fall back into place.

Epilogue

ONE YEAR LATER

Summer settled softly over Malta, warm and golden, the air rich with the smell of sea salt and citrus blossoms drifting in from the orchard. Noah stepped back from the newly painted shutters, the last pair finally done, and rested his arm against the sun-warmed stone. The house gleamed, every inch touched by his hands. His hands and one pair of far gentler ones. From the garden came Belle's laughter — light, content, unhurried. The sound had become the quiet pulse of his days. She knelt beside a bed of lavender, coaxing the young plants into place, her straw hat shielding her from the sun, her dress fluttering in the breeze.

The garden had been her idea. His dream, but her gift. Max bounded through the rosemary bushes, followed by a tiny ball of black-and-white fluff who tripped over its own oversized ears. Pippa, the newest member of their little household, rescued from a litter found behind the marina, yipped determinedly and tumbled into Max's side. The older dog tolerated her with saintly patience.

'Someone's teaching her bad habits,' Noah called from the terrace.

'It's called personality development,' Belinda answered without looking up.

'You let her steal a whole pastizzi yesterday.'

'She was *exploring her cultural heritage.*' He laughed, shaking his head. Life was… simple. A word neither of them had realized they'd been craving.

Belinda paused to stretch her back and looked around the garden, their garden, with a soft fullness in her chest. Raised beds brimming with herbs; citrus trees heavy with ripening fruit; bougainvillea climbing the old stone archway in a riot of pink. A year ago, she'd walked into this house heartbroken and unsure, but now she felt rooted, grounded and loved.

She brushed soil from her hands just as her phone pinged with a message: a picture from Susan, smiling, elegant, sitting beside a shy, neatly dressed man named Robert from her book club. *"Lunch with Robert. He insisted on paying. Should I be worried?"* it read. Belinda grinned and sent back: *'I think that's absolutely fine.'* Susan's heart, long bruised, long quiet, was learning to beat for someone new. Gently and cautiously.

Annalise and Jake, meanwhile, were still somewhere between luxury flights and boardrooms, sending sun-soaked photos from their honeymoon-that-never-ended. They had shocked everyone by choosing the simplest, sweetest ceremony imaginable, a quiet evening on a Hawaiian beach, barefoot in the sand. Jason had surprised Belinda too, finding his way back to Alicia. Communication, the thing she always struggled with, had become his new skill. They were taking it slow. Talking honestly. Healing.

And Carla… oh, Carla. Still, she insisted she wasn't

moving to Malta, while visiting Anton every month and developing an encyclopedic knowledge of his timetables. Belinda gave her three months, four at most, before she caved and shipped her shoe collection over permanently.

Mikiel remained unchangeable — part philosopher, part fisherman, part menace to every tourist who underestimated him in a Boċċi match. He came by twice a week with fresh fish and unsolicited advice in equal measure.

Everything in Belinda's world had shifted. Yet somehow felt entirely right.

That evening, the terrace flickered with candlelight. The table was set with Belinda's favourite dishes: hand-rolled ravioli stuffed with ġbejna and mint, grilled sea bream with lemon, fresh bread still warm from the oven. Noah wiped his palms on a tea towel; his heart was somehow both steady and wild. He'd rehearsed this. He'd scrapped the speech. Rehearsed again. Scrapped it again, but none of it mattered.Belinda stepped onto the terrace, glowing in a soft sundress, her hair loose around her shoulders. Her eyes warmed when she saw the table. 'Noah… it's beautiful.'

'You're early,' he teased. 'I was hoping for five more minutes to panic.'

She laughed, coming to him, wrapping her arms around his waist. 'About what?'

'About this,' he murmured as he reached into his pocket. Belinda stilled as Noah dropped to one knee. Candlelight flickered across his face, earnest, loving, and more than a little nervous.

'Belle… I've spent this past year learning the difference between existing and living.' His voice was soft and steady. 'And I don't want a single day of living without you.' Her breath caught. 'Will you marry me?'

The sea whispered against the rocks below, Pippa

barked and Max thumped his tail. Belinda's eyes filled, her smile trembling into place like sunrise breaking across a horizon. 'Yes,' she whispered. 'Of course I will.'

Noah exhaled hard, half laugh, half relief, as she pulled him up and kissed him, slow and certain. The candles flickered as the night wrapped around them, warm and sweet.

And everything, absolutely everything, was right.

Next in the Sublime Retreats Romance Series

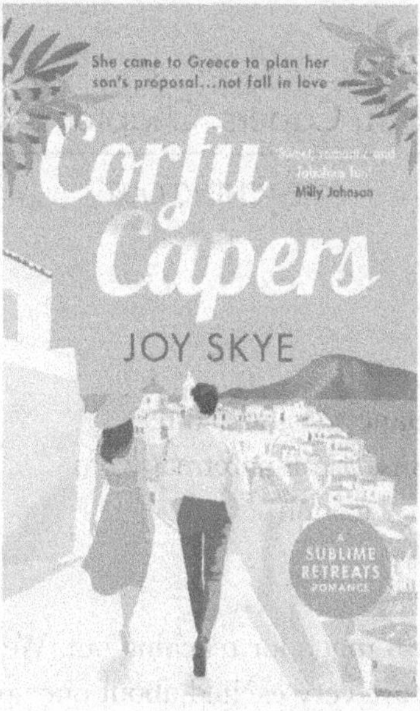

vinci-books.com/corfu-capers

Can a holiday heal a broken heart?

Divorcée Kate Delaney heads to Corfu to plan her son's perfect proposal and prove she's fine solo. When her careful plans collapse, the island's warmth and charming male resident, Pericles, pull her into unexpected possibilities. Maybe this holiday holds the second chance her heart still craves.

Turn the page for a free preview…

Corfu Capers: Chapter One

REACHING OUT

From: KateDelaney@yahoo.com
To: PeterWilliams@sublimeretreats.com
Subject: Corfu Vacation

Dear Peter,

Thank you so much for reaching out. We are all looking forward to and are very excited about our upcoming trip to Corfu next month.

It will be myself, my son Scott and his girlfriend Linda, plus their two friends, Marc and Charlotte, staying at the villa. I will forward the grocery list requested shortly; I just have to double-check everybody's allergies. Please have all the beds made up as doubles.

We arrive at 10 am on the Aegean flight from Athens, and will be spending two nights there en route. Can you recommend a hotel and a guide? We would like to see as much as possible whilst we are in the capital.

We will need a transfer when we land in Corfu. I don't like the idea of my son having to drive all the way to the villa when we first arrive. We need a vehicle big enough for the 5 of us plus lots of luggage; can you get a limousine there?

You see, this is going to be a very special trip; my son is going to propose to his girlfriend!

I am so excited and can't wait to plan everything. I need your help to come up with the perfect spot for this event and arrange for a photographer to be in place to snap the momentous occasion. This will happen on Thursday after we have had a few days to settle in.

Scott doesn't know this, but I have also invited 15 of our friends and relatives to come and celebrate with us. They will be staying at The Bella Mare hotel in Avlaki, which is just down the road from the villa, I believe, so will be very convenient for coordination purposes.

After the proposal, I would adore it if we could all go to a restaurant for a celebratory meal. Once I have decided on a suitable venue, I will leave it to you to make all the arrangements. Can we have some decorations, maybe some flowers, balloons, etc.? I would also love to provide our guests with rose petals to throw as the couple walk in? And, of course, we will need champagne, preferably Dom Perignon, if that's possible? If you have any other ideas on how to make this vacation beyond special, please let me know.

I look forward to hearing your ideas for my plan and, by the way, are we safe to drink the tap water on Corfu?

Best regards,

Ms Kate Delaney

From: PeterWilliams@sublimeretreats.com

To: KateDelaney@yahoo.com
Subject: Corfu Vacation

Dear Kate,

It was lovely to hear from you and I am thrilled to help you organise such an amazing event. It's going to be fabulous!

We do not have limousines on Corfu, I'm afraid, but I can offer you a luxury minibus transfer that will very comfortably accommodate your party and its luggage. The cost will be €300 each way; if this is acceptable, I shall go ahead and book?

Given the location of your villa I believe I know the perfect spot for your son to propose, there is a wonderful restaurant on the beach below called Cavo Barbaro and directly in front of it is a jetty with incredible views beyond (thinking Instagram moment here) which would be perfect. The photographer could discreetly sit at the restaurant and catch the moment from there. It is also within walking distance for your 'secret' guests to come and join the celebration afterwards.

I can arrange to have the restaurant decorated in advance and have a special table booked for you and your guests. Yes, I can provide Dom Perignon for you. How many bottles shall I order?

Please find attached a selection of trips and tours I can recommend to you to make the most of your stay on Corfu. We can also organise for one of our wonderful local chefs to come and cook at the villa one evening, maybe on the last night, so you can enjoy the amazing views from the villa terrace for your final meal.

We do not recommend drinking the tap water here. It is not dangerous, but it has a high mineral content that can upset your stomach, so I shall add bottled water to your grocery list when it comes through.

Please let me know if I can assist with anything else to make your stay as memorable as possible.

Regards

Peter

Sublime Retreats Concierge

Peter, who was sitting in his lounge as he read his emails, pulled out his diary from his bag and started scheduling the plans for Ms. Delaney's upcoming trip. The guests who were currently staying in the villa he looked after were remarkably low maintenance, and he was feeling decidedly unwanted. Every time he paid them a visit, he could barely get through the door. Mind you, judging by the photos the maid had shown him of the array of adult toys in the bedside table, it wasn't totally surprising that they didn't want his company. He didn't know what half of the devices were for, and some of them he definitely didn't want to know.

He was pretty sure they had been skinny dipping the first day he visited, hastily arranged sarongs giving the game away and not particularly disguising anything, so he now tactfully beeped his horn on arrival to give them the opportunity to cover up their sun toasted parts.

Ms Delaney, however, would appear to be much more his cup of tea. Her list of requirements would keep him busy right up until she arrived and beyond, which was how he liked it. Being essential to his guest's plans was his raison d'être.

He loved his job with Sublime Retreats; their exclusive membership and exorbitant joining fee guaranteed all his guests were noteworthy, high-end travellers, and being able to respond to their ever-increasing demands was his passion, some would even say his life. As the emails from guests came in on a daily basis leading up to their arrival, he devoured each one like it was a personal challenge, scouring them for clues and looking for opportunities to go above and beyond his fundamental concierge role.

His friends and colleagues were constantly ribbing him for his attention to detail and overkill in pre-empting his guest's needs, but, let's face it, his customer service scores and his weekly tips spoke for themselves. He knew this resulted in him being the centre of idle gossip and bitchy comments in the office and his best friend Emma, who also worked there, was always having to defend him. It did hurt his feelings, but he tried to let it go over his head.

He and Alex, his partner, had moved to Corfu 10 years before, deciding that a more relaxed way of life was in order after being made redundant forced him to re-evaluate his priorities. They had been holidaying on the island, in the resort of Arillas on the west coast, for years and had often idly talked about their dream of moving there over a late-night glass of wine on their balcony overlooking the sea. After weeks of job searching and agonising, the pipe dream they'd always had seemed to make more sense than wasting away their lives in the London humdrum. So they made the break, selling up their flat and escaping to the sun and a more carefree way of life.

Peter had settled straight into the relaxed vibe of Corfu, despite the frustrations they came across with buying a property there. The red tape and paperwork seemed to go on forever and require a different person to stamp it at every stage. He'd made his first port of call to sign up for Greek lessons, which is where he had met Emma. He applied the same method and determination to learning this new language as he did to everything else in his life, and his language skills soon surpassed her own, despite her having been learning for several years. But they remained great friends and when the job came up at her office, she forced him to send in his CV, knowing he would be perfect for the job role. And she was right; he'd taken to it like a duck to water.

Alex, however, seemed to take no pleasure from their new surroundings, and any attempt he made at learning Greek was in the bar, where he learned to order another round quite easily. He managed to hold down a job for a while with one of the cheap end UK tour operators that had hotels there, but his newfound lethargy seeped into his work and his contract wasn't renewed for the next season.

When Alex died without warning two years ago, after 15 years together, Peter had been devastated and completely unprepared for this seeming desertion. So, throwing himself into his work had been his salvation. He found that his work distracted him from the loneliness and helped him to avoid the otherwise inevitable drive back to the empty house that no longer felt like home, despite the affection from his two spoiled cats, Samson and Delilah.

Now, slowly but surely, he was opening up to the idea that there could be someone else for him, somewhere. But living on a small Greek island where opinions were around 30 years out of date made it impossible to be openly gay. It wasn't the same as London where he knew the bars and clubs where he would be welcomed.

Still, he'd been pleasantly surprised when he downloaded the Grindr app a few weeks ago, after months of indecision, to discover plenty of possibilities within the community on there. He hadn't been brave enough yet to meet up with anyone, but it made him feel better that he did have options close to home. He scrolled through daily and a couple of people had caught his eye. Any day now he would click on a profile and see where it led, but not just yet.

Peter sent a quick message to the photographer he liked to use, Lucy, to tell her to pencil in the date and to give her a rough sketch of the plan so far. He knew he'd have to keep reminding her as she was a bit ditsy, but her work was fantastic and his guests were always thrilled with the results, so she was worth the extra effort involved. He was already envisaging 'the moment', as he had mentally labelled the proposal, and couldn't wait to make it happen.

He loved the diversity of the requests he received every week in his work. From sourcing and importing unique brands of bottled water, finding Greek dancers to entertain the guests in the villas, and organising wild off-road bike tours, to his ultimate request, he felt, finding a landing spot nearby for the private helicopter that brought in one set of guests. That had been a real feather in his cap when he had managed to convince the local council to let them land at the kids' football pitch on the outskirts of Kassiopi, saving his customers the hour-long drive from the airport for which they were very grateful and he was tipped handsomely.

Peter checked the time and, realising he needed to get on the road, stood up and walked over to the kitchen to open some food for his cats. Hearing the sound of a tin pop open, they both rushed in and wound themselves around his legs until he managed to empty the food into their bowls without tripping over them.

'You two love me, don't you guys? ' he said, rubbing their heads before grabbing his tablet, diary and work bag and setting out to the office, planning to stop first at the restaurant he had in mind for 'the moment' and the party afterwards. He wanted to start making the arrangements and see what extra mile he could go to, so this would be an experience to remember for all involved. He couldn't wait to tell Emma about his latest request, being stuck in the office dealing with accounts for most of the day; she loved to live vicariously through what she saw as his more glamorous role.

Kate Delany was sitting in the reading nook of her tastefully decorated English style house in Houston when she read Peter's email; he sounded as if he was the perfect concierge and, combined with her amazing planning skills, this should be a vacation to remember.

She glanced around the room, looking at the rows of romance novels she avidly read, memories floating across her mind of all the happy hours she'd spent there. Maybe she should sell up now that Scott was going to be married and living elsewhere? Although he'd moved out years ago when he first started work, he still spent a lot of time with his mum, keeping her company regularly and joining her every Sunday without fail for lunch. The house was too big for her alone and she knew that with the money she would make from selling it she could buy herself a suitable apartment in pretty much any area she liked, but as yet she hadn't made any real effort to put this idea into action.

She supposed she would see a lot less of her son after the wedding, which worried her, but the fact that her ex-husband was none too keen on their son's choice of girlfriend did make up for that a little. She couldn't wait to hear his reaction to their son's engagement to Linda Garcia. He was gonna have a duck fit and no mistake.

She had met and fallen for Danial Delaney at the Lankford Grocery Store when he was a lowly errand boy. She had been swept off her feet, captivated by his good looks and charm and, for the first time in her life, began to disobey her abusive father by sneaking out at night and meeting Danial whenever she could. After years of constant maltreatment and being made to feel that she was no better than dirt, the stolen hours with him were magical and addictive, and she couldn't wait to marry him as soon as it was legal, on her 18th birthday in the courthouse in the next town.

The intense scene that followed when they went back home to tell her family of the marriage was one she'd never forget. Her father was convulsed with a rage beyond anything she had experienced before, screaming that Danial was 'lower than a snake's belly', his face turning purple with fury, veins popping alarmingly as he hissed that Danial would never have a pot to piss in and that they could go and live in the ghetto as they deserved. When he started hurling insults at Kate, Danial had to be restrained and she'd dragged her new husband out of the house and away from her family home forever.

Her father had disowned her straight away and forbade any member of the family, including her mother, from having any contact with her, so her new husband had become her entire world. But she had been living in a bubble of love and joy and when she fell pregnant soon after, her life was complete; making a family and creating a home for the two men in her life in the tiny one-bedroom apartment they first had when they were 'too poor to paint, too proud to whitewash', as her grandmother used to say.

Danial, with his magnetism and boyish good looks, had gone on to found one of the largest real estate companies in Texas, and over the course of the years, they had moved up the property chain. When he opened his fifth office, they bought the wonderful house in Cinco Ranch, an area she had always loved and aspired to. Its leafy streets and suburban feel, along with the cachet of the community with the expensive shops and restaurants, made her feel that they had really made it and showed her Pa once and for all that she had made the right decision.

Even though her husband seemed to be working longer and longer hours and be away on frequent trips, she appreciated his reasoning that he just wanted to provide everything he could for her and their son, always bearing armfuls of presents on his return to salve any wounds left by his constant absences. She had been so very happy in her role as homemaker and mother; she hadn't given it a second thought.

When Danial had abandoned them, her world fell apart and her focus became concentrated entirely on her son; it was the only way she could cope and get through day to day, and she thanked the lord that her father was no longer alive to gloat at her misfortune as he surely would have. As time went by, the pain lessened and, after the shockingly quick divorce and the healthy settlement Danial had agreed to without demur, which included the house, she began to rebuild her life.

Scott continued to be her entire world, but as he got older and naturally spent more time away from the house, first with friends, then girls and then college, she had found she needed to fill her days and try and combat the loneliness. Even though she had been reacquainted with her family after her father's death, she didn't have any real women friends and certainly no boyfriends; she could never trust anybody enough again to let them that close. So she had joined a couple of women's groups before discovering local charities, clamouring out for women just like her. With plenty of free time and a passion for organising, she soon became in demand to organise various events and fundraisers.

She had become particularly involved with two of Houston's women's shelters, providing safety and a new start for women and their children that had been victims of abuse, and she had raised thousands of Dollars for them with various fundraisers as well as contributing as many hours as she could at the shelters.

Thinking ahead to the future, to after this holiday and a life not devoted to Scott, she realised she needed to find a new purpose in life, something that would engage even more of her time and combat the loneliness she sometimes felt. She had no idea what it might be that would assuage the feelings of remoteness from the rest of the world, but she knew she needed to be part of something else when her family life became scaled down.

She roused herself from her reverie and walked through to the inviting country-style kitchen that she had enjoyed planning and creating so much. The room was large and airy, the wood on the high beamed ceiling complimenting the work surface she had chosen and contrasting with the pale cream cupboards. At the far end, where the large double doors opened to the conservatory, she had placed two wonderful, overstuffed sofas that made the space seem cosier, and the room had become the hub of their family life.

She turned on the Nespresso machine lined up on the counter with her many other gadgets. "I wonder if the villa has one of these," she thought to herself and made a mental note to keep a checklist of things to ask that lovely concierge before they flew out.

She was interrupted from her thoughts by her phone

ringing. Dan Gillespie Sells' 'My Boy', identifying it as Scott before she dug it out from the depth of her Fendi handbag.

'Good Morning my gorgeous boy, how are you today?' she enquired with a big smile on her face as she placed her cup in the slot and pressed the button to set the coffee machine in action with its familiar buzz.

'Howdy Ma, I'm fine, thought I'd check-in. How are your plans for Corfu going? I'm getting a little nervous now, I have to admit.'

'Don't you worry about a thing. I will make sure it all runs smoothly and everything is absolutely perfect for you both. You know I won't let anything spoil it for you.'

Scott chuckled to himself 'I have no doubt regards to that Ma, none at all. It's Linda that I worry about. What if she says no? What if she doesn't like the ring? I'm as nervous as a long-tailed cat in a roomful of rocking chairs.'

'Now you listen to me, Scotty,' she said as she carried her cup carefully to the table, phone wedged between her ear and shoulder 'that girl will be lucky to have you as a husband and if she's got an iota of sense, she knows that. And she will be lucky to have a Mother in Law who cares enough to plan all this for her, so she should be more than grateful. As for the ring, it cost so much she can't not love it, it's stunning.'

His eyes instantaneously flicked to the mantelpiece in his lounge, where the velvet blue box containing the ring was presently sitting. His paranoia regarding losing it had made him neurotic, and he was constantly checking it was still in there.

'OK, OK, don't get yer dander up; I just get a little jittery is all. Can you forward me all the flight details so I can let Marc and Charlotte know the timings? I'm so glad they're both coming along. It will make the whole trip a lot easier'

'It will be nice for Linda to have her best friend there to enjoy the special moment, but as for that playboy friend of yours Marc, you will have to watch him, I trust him as far as I can spit which ain't that far. You know Charlotte has always had a soft spot for him and I can handle her being all doe-eyed at the breakfast table, but not heartbroken. You can tell him from me to keep his manicured paws to himself. If he needs to let off steam, he can head into the village and charm a local peasant girl.'

Scott, sitting on his balcony overlooking Market Square Park, laughed out loud at his mother's fierceness. He knew her well enough to know she was predominantly concerned about her grand plan rather than poor Charlotte's wellbeing.

'Message received loud and clear, Ma'am; I'll give him his instructions. You never can tell, he may be swept off his feet by a luscious local beauty'

'I will believe that when I see it, that boy is a confirmed bachelor if ever I saw one. He cares far too much for his looks to have time for anyone else, as his track record to date shows. He never goes out with the same girl twice.'

'True enough. Are we still on for dinner tonight?' he said, changing the subject abruptly. 'I said I'd pick Linda up from the salon when she finishes at six and head straight over? She's looking forward to going through all the final travel plans with you.'

'Yes, that's fine; I'm making your favourite, linguine with shrimp'

'You do remember Linda is allergic to seafood, Ma?'

'Oh yes, I keep forgetting. Well, I'm sure I can rustle

something else up for her. My boy deserves his favourite meal once in a while.'

Scott hung up the phone to his Mother, shaking his head as he walked back into his apartment to get some breakfast. Her organisational skills were renown throughout Houston. The fact that she insisted on organising his life wasn't something he was so keen on, but he understood. He understood that when his father left his mother for a cliché younger model all those years ago; he became the centre of her world, and her desire to be in control overtook her desire for anything else. She threw herself into organising his life as much as the charities she volunteered for on a regular basis.

He knew Linda found it tough to deal with, as had his previous girlfriends, and he was hoping that this trip would bring the women in his life closer together, or at least give them a better understanding of each other. He adored Linda and couldn't imagine a life without her in it, and was determined to make this work. When he had admitted to Kate that he was thinking to propose, she'd pounced on the idea with vengeance and had steamrollered things until now, a few short months later, he was on the brink of making the biggest commitment of his life on a beach in Corfu and he was feeling a little shell-shocked.

Tapping with practised ease at the screen of his phone, he messaged Linda to confirm the plans for the evening, tactfully suggesting she should have a big lunch in the hope that she wouldn't be too hungry when they went for dinner that night.

He finished his cereal, rinsing the bowl and placing it neatly in the dishwasher before checking the ring again and then putting it in his briefcase and heading out for his morning's property viewings. He had big hopes of shifting that imposing five-bed property in River Oaks before going on vacation so he could hit his sales target for this month and earn another bonus. His father had already messaged three times that morning to remind him of the importance of this sale, as if he needed more pressure laid on him at this point.

Working at his dad's real estate firm was something he enjoyed but, as the boss's son, he felt a real pressure to be the top salesman. He knew the other members of staff assumed he had it easy, but in reality, when he saw his father, which was periodically, Danial Delaney was a lot harder on Scott than anyone else in the firm. The burden of living up to his father's entrepreneurial talents was constant and, if he was honest, was also spurred by his need for approval from the man who abandoned them all those years ago.

Despite his growing nerves regarding proposing to Linda, he was looking forward to taking a real break, the first one he'd allowed himself since he'd started working at the firm six years before. In some ways, he wished he could take a longer break. A week didn't seem long enough to truly relax, especially under the circumstances. He really should look at taking more time out for himself. Maybe Linda would appreciate it if they took a quick holiday in the fall; he'd have to ask her if she'd like that.

Linda glanced down at her phone when the screen flashed and saw it was a message from Scott. No doubt confirming darling Mummy's plans for tonight, she thought a little sharply. She gave herself a mental shake and focused on massaging the hands in front of her. As a nail artist in Houston's busiest salon, she had back-to-back appointments all day with a scant 20 minutes for lunch if she was lucky.

But it paid a reasonable salary, the tips were good and, for the most part, she enjoyed her work. She liked meeting new people and hearing all about their lives. Everyone else seemed to have a life full of adventure and travel, and she longed to be like them.

She hadn't told anyone, not even her best friend Charlotte, but she'd started saving up in what she liked to call her 'possibilities pot' five years back, where she put all her tips. She now had a nest egg that she knew meant she could travel wherever she wanted and spent many happy hours online checking out destinations. She had a plan of her route mapped out, which would involve travelling for around ten months, but was unsure if she was brave enough to take that chunk of time out of her life. It seemed an impossible dream in many ways, but it was a dream that would not go away and she cherished it, keeping it close to her heart, and it fuelled the more tedious parts of her day.

If she was honest with herself, her desire to travel was the main reason she'd agreed to go on this vacation with Scott's mum. That and the fact they said she could bring Charlotte with her. It would be unbearable otherwise. She was sure having her best friend to gripe about Kate to would make all the difference. She wasn't sure if she and Scott were right for each other. He seemed so focused on his work above anything else, and she longed to be free. It didn't seem such a good match, but the fact he'd agreed to some time away had surprised her and made her feel that she should give it a little longer before making any permanent decisions about their relationship.

She understood why Kate was so hung up on her son, but he was 30 now, for God's sake, time to let go! Her constant interfering in his life could be so oppressive sometimes, and Linda had to bite her tongue regularly to avoid conflict with her boyfriend. She was looking forward to grabbing some quality time with him while they were away and had applied online to get International Driving Permits for them both so they could make use of the hire car and explore by themselves. She hoped that Kate would loosen her apron strings enough to allow this to happen, but had her doubts.

She finished up her appointment with Mrs Howser, who came in every week to see her and ran to Starbucks to grab a coffee and a sandwich. It was then that she read the message from Scott, advising a large lunch, which, reading between the lines, meant Kate had 'accidentally' forgotten about her seafood allergy yet again. She sighed to herself and finished up her lunch before running back to work. Marc was coming in this afternoon for his regular manicure and she always enjoyed seeing him.

Of all Scott's friends, he was the only one she felt she could talk to, who understood her frustrations with Kate's overbearing nature and her boyfriend's refusal to stand up to it. The boys had been friends since they were toddlers and Marc had seen the disruption caused when Scott's dad had left and the effect it had had on his mum. Even though they had chosen to go to different colleges, Scott to study Business administration and Marc to study Veterinary medicine, their friendship had remained rock solid and they had stayed best friends.

You would think after three years of going out with Scott that she would be used to Kate by now, but it was becoming increasingly irritating. Her controlling behaviour still managed to exasperate her and make her feel helpless, as there was nothing she could seemingly do about it without causing an argument. Never mind, just a few more days to go and they'd be on their way, travelling to Europe, to Greece no less and what looked like the most idyllic island there. She couldn't wait.

Corfu Capers: Chapter Two

THE PLOT THICKENS

From: KateDelaney@yahoo.com
To: PeterWilliams@sublimeretreats.com
Subject: Corfu Vacation

Dear Peter,

Please go ahead and book the luxury minibus transfer. I assume it is air-conditioned? How will we find the driver when we arrive at Corfu airport?

Your suggestions for the proposal location sound absolutely marvellous. I've checked out the restaurant online and it all looks too good to be true. Please go ahead and book everything we have discussed.

I have confirmed the reservations for my 15 guests that are staying at the hotel. I will forward all their flight details tomorrow. Could you be a darling and book their taxis for them?

I love the look of the boat trip with Captain Yiannis; I believe he can take us along the coastline for the day? Please book that in for the Wednesday. Looking at his menu choices, I would love to request the seafood option for our group. I would also like to take up your suggestion for a chef at the villa for the last night, which sounds ideal. Please forward their menu and I will let you know what we choose for all the courses.

I have attached the grocery list of things we would like in place for our arrival. Please add 10 bottles of my favourite wine Whispering Angel to that list and make sure they are refrigerated, along with the water.

With regards to the champagne for the celebration, I think twenty bottles should suffice, even for my family.

Can you also let me know what type of coffee machine they have there and make sure to add the appropriate pods or whatever to the list?

There are no food allergies in our group to be of concern.

Is there anything else that you believe is a must-do whilst we are in Corfu? We only have a week there and whilst I don't want to be running around for the whole trip, I certainly don't want us to miss anything either.

I gather from your emails that most of your suppliers prefer to be paid in cash. Is it safe to walk around with large amounts of money over there? I wouldn't dream of it here.

Best regards,

Ms Kate Delaney

From: PeterWilliams@sublimeretreats.com
To: KateDelaney@yahoo.com
Subject: Corfu Vacation

Dear Kate,

Yes, the luxury minivans are air-conditioned. Your driver will meet you inside the arrival hall bearing a sign with your name on it. He will assist you with your luggage and take you to the transfer vehicle. I will meet you at the villa and give you an orientation of the house so that you know how everything works and can settle straight in.

I have your grocery list and will ensure everything will be in place for your arrival, but please note, we do not have 'half and half', granola or pastrami. I will substitute with local produce for you to try. I am sure you will enjoy them. The villa has a Nespresso machine, so I will order a selection of pods for you and your guests.

Everything is organised for the proposal. I have booked the restaurant that we decided on, ordered the decorations and I am meeting with Lucy, the photographer, later today just to make sure we're all on the same page.

I will be delighted to book the taxis for your hotel guests as requested. Will they be paying individually?

You have a busy week lined up with us, but I would recommend you spend some time in Corfu Town before you leave. It is absolutely beautiful and full of amazing history; I could show you around if you want to spend an afternoon there. There is also a wonderful wine tasting tour at our local vineyard that I feel you would enjoy.

I see from your notes you have hired a car with Zeus Cars to be delivered to the villa. I will call them to confirm and make sure they know where to come. Please note that if you are expecting an automatic, most of the cars here are stick shift. It might be worth double-checking with them before you arrive as automatics are in short supply. Shall I do this for you?

With regard to cash, Corfu has a very low crime rate, but I would still advise caution when out and about and using the safety deposit boxes provided in your villa. There are several ATMs in the area so we can arrange for you to take out cash as and when you need it rather than bringing it with you. It's a good idea to advise your bank that you will be travelling to avoid any problems. Another point to note is that Amex cards don't always work here for some reason.

I think we have everything in place. Let me know if you feel we are missing anything.

Regards,

Peter

Peter Williams

Sublime Retreats Concierge

The night before they were due to leave, Linda received a message from Scott saying that he was working late and would have to cancel their dinner plans again. Shaking her head, she finished packing her suitcase and gave Charlotte a call. She wanted to chat to her friend about Marc before they left anyway, so now was a good opportunity.

'Hi hun, do you fancy grabbing a bite to eat tonight? I have absolutely nothing left to eat here and Scotty is working late yet again.'

'That boy works far too hard, but I guess you shouldn't complain. Food sounds like a good idea, though. I was just going to order a pizza, and I'd only end up eating the whole thing' she laughed 'shall we do our usual?'

Linda agreed and an hour later they met at their favourite restaurant, which was within walking distance for both of them. As they walked into the gaily decorated Tex

Mex, with its bright orange, colour-washed walls and the inevitable sombreros delineating every booth, they both felt a surge of excitement, knowing they didn't have to go to work tomorrow and the adventure that lay ahead, they started talking ten to the dozen, chattering over each other in a flurry of conversation.

'I can't wait for tomorrow' said Charlotte, her eyes shining with excitement as she sipped the margarita she'd ordered while deciding what to eat, looking carefully through the menu for the least fattening meals.

'I hope that excitement is due to your sense of adventure rather than your sense of getting up close and personal with Marc' stated Linda, nervously twisting her St. Christopher necklace, deciding to get straight to the point.

'I have no idea what you are talking about,' Charlotte replied, leaning forward to take a sip of her drink. 'I am in no mood to be getting it on with anyone right now. No matter what a gorgeous hunk of a man they may be, I have just split up with that idiot Jason. I only want to swim, sunbathe and relax for a while.'

Linda, who couldn't quite believe Charlotte's innocent expression, narrowed her eyes and carried on, determined to push her point home.

'I know Marc is gorgeous, but you know how he is. He's all hat an' no cattle as far as women are concerned and the last thing you need. I want you to promise me that you are not going to try anything while we are away and if I see you acting up, I'm gonna jerk a knot in your tail!'

She looked so fierce that Charlotte couldn't help but laugh 'don't you worry about little ol' me' she said, smiling at her best friend and, a decision made, putting her menu to one side 'I think you should be more concerned with the antics of Ms D ruining this trip. How was dinner with her the other night?'

'The woman is unbelievable. First, off she cooked shrimp, which I can't eat, so my "dinner"' she said sarcastically, with exaggerated air quotes 'was a grilled cheese sandwich'

'Well, at least she fed ya something,' Charlotte said, smiling at the waiter who came to take their orders. 'What about all her other plans?' she continued after he'd left.

'God knows, she was very circumspect with what she has planned beyond the flight details, apparently, we will find out when we get there. She really gets my goose with all this cloak and dagger nonsense.'

'Are you sure you're gonna manage a whole week with the woman?' Charlotte asked her friend as their fajitas were placed in front of them.

'It's not going to be easy for sure,' said Linda, rolling her eyes. 'Thank God you're gonna be there. If I look as if I'm going to kill her, drag me off and throw me in the pool to calm down,' she laughed.

They finished off their meal with delicious Churro Cheesecakes dusted liberally with cinnamon and a coffee to counteract the margaritas they'd consumed before kissing each other goodnight and going their separate ways.

It was later that night, when she was brushing her teeth before bed, that Linda suddenly realised that Charlotte had not made her that promise about Marc. 'Dang that girl,' she thought to herself as she climbed into bed. 'I hope she heeds my advice.'

Charlotte's eyes snapped open two seconds before the alarm went off. "Today's the day," she thought, feeling like it was Christmas morning. "Today is the first day of the rest of my life when I become Mrs Marc Miller.". She'd had her sights on him since the first day she'd clapped eyes on him and now she would finally have her chance. A whole week with Marc in a stunning villa in Greece; what could be more romantic? She envisioned him becoming more entranced with her as the week unfolded, the ambience of the stunning Greek island setting the mood for a full-blown romance to erupt.

This was the chance she had been waiting for, and she was going to make the most of it. She'd spent the best part of two months' salary on an entirely new wardrobe for the trip, although as a children's swim coach at the local pool she didn't earn a fortune. She was determined to knock his socks off and make him forget the never-ending trail of girls he seemed to have on his arm every time she saw him.

She had met Marc the same fateful night that Linda had met Scott. They had been on a girl's night out at Etro nightclub, dancing off her blues at splitting up with yet another hapless boyfriend, letting the 80s music lift her spirits and letting their hair down as they danced the night away. She had gone to the bar looking for Linda, who had disappeared sometime before to get some drinks and found her chatting to two good-looking men, who were leaning on the bar drinking whisky, looking very laid back and suave.

Her eyes were drawn straight away to the taller of the two, his thick black hair, the fringe falling expertly over his bright blue eyes just so, and his sensuous mouth smiling in greeting as she walked up. She'd panicked then, thinking how frightful she must look, hot and sweaty after their recent frenzied dance to Girls Just Want To Have Fun. She made her excuses and ran to the sanctuary of the bathroom, the subtle lighting doing nothing to help as she despaired at what the mirror revealed. She did her best to adjust her hair, reapplied her lip gloss and straightened out her top, which had shifted during all the jigging around.

Charlotte was insecure with regards to her looks, despite Linda's constant reassurances and the obvious effect she had on men. Her mother and elder sister had both been Prom queens, always the belles of the ball, and she had grown up feeling dowdy by comparison. Her natural tomboy leanings as a child, always happiest in jeans and preferably covered in mud, provoking their derision and merciless teasing until eventually, as a teenager, she had gradually fallen into line. Now she couldn't bear to leave the house until she looked as perfect as she could be.

That night they had both left the club alone, but whereas Linda's relationship with Scott had blossomed, Marc had put her firmly, and seemingly permanently, in the friend zone, something she had resolved to change this week.

She pushed aside the covers and bounced out of bed, stumbling sleepily towards the bathroom to shower. It was 4 am, two hours before she had to leave her apartment, but she was determined to look her best when they all met at the airport, which was gonna take some fixin'.

When they met at the United Airlines check-in desk in terminal C at George Bush Intercontinental a few hours later, Charlotte was dressed to kill. Her long blonde hair had been blow-dried to perfection, bouncing in the manner of a shampoo advert with every step she took. Her eyes were made up to maximise their wonderful shade of blue and emphasise her long lashes, her lips were glossed and her heels were roughly 3 inches too high to be practical for a long day of travelling.

Linda pulled her to one side. 'What the hell are you playing at?' she demanded. 'I thought we had agreed that

Marc was out of bounds for the duration of this vacation. Those pants are so tight I can see your religion!'

Charlotte crossed her arms.'You may have agreed that but I most certainly did not,' she declared adamantly and slightly smugly, Linda thought.

'Don't be stupid' snapped Linda, rolling her eyes. 'now change out of those ridiculous shoes into something more sensible before we check in our bags. God knows when we'll see them again.'

Eventually, they were organised, Charlotte's minor concession being slightly lower heels, and they had checked in and made it through security to begin the first leg of their journey. They had a long flight ahead plus a two-hour layover at Frankfurt before they got to Athens. Linda looked over at Scott and Kate, who were standing to one side talking, and she felt unsettled.

She was sure that Kate was up to something; she was getting a strange vibe from the woman that was making her feel uncomfortable. Fair enough, she'd organised and paid for the whole trip, but the covert muttering in corners and constant glances were beginning to get to Linda, and she didn't care for it. And Scott seemed to have developed a nervous tic of some description; he kept patting the side pocket of his carry-on bag as if it was some kind of talisman.

'What's going on' she demanded of Scott when she'd pried him away to queue up at Peet's Coffee & Tea to get drinks for everyone before they boarded. 'Why are you and mummy dearest huddling in corners at every available opportunity?'

'I have no idea what you are talking about, honey. Now try to relax and let's enjoy this vacation. My Ma and me are just relishing some time together, pay us no mind. What coffee do you want?' he said absently, looking at his phone at yet another message from Danial about the River Oaks deal.

'Oh, I think I'd better have a Latte Macchiato, make it a large one,' she said, feeling wrong-footed by his casual reply.

Perhaps she was being paranoid, she thought to herself as they walked back towards the others through the miasma of perfume coming from Duty-Free, overthinking things with Scott and maybe her friend Charlotte too. She'd have to try and relax and get into holiday mode. After all, in a few minutes, she would be getting on a plane and going somewhere new, something she had been hankering for all of her life. She couldn't let Kate Delaney spoil this.

Peter was waiting in the luxurious reception of the Bella Mare hotel for the first influx of Ms Delaney's extra guests. It wasn't his job in reality, as they weren't staying at the villa, but he had nothing better to do, despite it being a Saturday night, and he felt it would make a good impression. He knew he was going beyond his job spec, but he didn't care. Little touches like this made all the difference.

He checked his phone for the time and estimated the first taxis should be there in approximately five minutes if there had been no delays. Whilst he was looking at his phone, it chimed and a notification from Grindr popped up. Someone had messaged him! He paused for a second, closing his eyes briefly before he opened the app. It was a simple 'Hi, how are you?' which was a relief, as he'd received a few that had been far too direct for his liking.

He looked through the profile of George, a local waiter at a restaurant in Kassiopi. He looked nice enough and in the right age group, but Peter still wasn't 100% sure he was ready to get out there. He touched the flame icon to send a 'tap' to let George know he was interested but would message later. He'd need time to work out what to say for a start.

Peter returned to the main screen and was delighted to note there were 18 other users within 2km of him right at that second. He smiled in amazement and glanced up just in time to see the first taxi pulling into the driveway. Standing up, pulling his shirt into place and putting on his 'meet and greet' face, he strode out and down the steps to welcome the guests.

Forty minutes later it was chaos in the reception area as fifteen exhausted and, for the most part, elderly Texans tried to understand the Greek check-in process which was no more complicated than anywhere else in the world, but seemingly took a lot of talking about.

Bill and Bobby, who apparently were Ms Delaney's cousins and obviously twins, seemed to be arguing non stop, noisily, as if they were small children bickering between themselves over anything and everything.

'Pay them no mind' said Great Aunt Eustice, a neat, prim and proper old lady wearing a large straw hat decorated with fruit, who was gazing around with a look of utter distaste and looked like she was sucking a lemon.

'They may look the same, but they be two different buckets of possums.'

Shaking his head, Peter made his way to the front of the queue where Uncle Joe, an octogenarian who could benefit from the use of a hearing aid, seemed to be taking an inordinately long time.

'What seems to be the problem, Joe?' he asked and smiled at Vasso, the poor receptionist dealing with the arrival, letting her see that he sympathised with her and was there to help.

'She keeps wanting to charge me for sex,' Joe whispered,

having to reach up to Peter's ear, as he was a full head taller than the old man. 'She keeps telling me it's €3 a night for the room sex, which seems mighty cheap to me. I know the country is in financial straits, but even so.'

Taken aback, Peter spoke to Vasso in Greek to double-check the conversation. She answered in rapid-fire sentences and Peter began to laugh.

'Oh Joe, she's asking for the Room Tax,' he said, putting his hand on the man's shoulder. 'It's a local charge that has to be paid in cash; they can't put it on your bill.'

A big smile erupted on Joe's wrinkled face and he burst out laughing, clapped his hands together and proceeded to tell the rest of the group at top volume, adding 'I only hesitated because at my age I wasn't sure I'd get my money's worth!' and started laughing uproariously again as poor Vasso slowly went beetroot red as she realised what was being said.

Finally, they were all checked in and the bellboy was running back and forth, transporting the luggage to the various rooms, sweating under the weight. They all seemed to have packed for a month, not a week. Peter stood talking with Joe, as he seemed to be the unofficial leader of the group.

'Once you are all settled in, I have reserved a table at a taverna a few minutes' walk away for you'

'I hope it's not too far. Most of us can't walk for toffee,' laughed Joe amenably as they strolled towards the lift.

'It's 2 minutes,' said Peter, pressing the call button.

'Just turn left out of the gate and you'll see it right by the sea.'

Uncle Joe called the stragglers who hadn't gone to their rooms yet to squeeze into the small lift with him and jabbed at the button for his floor 'see you tomorrow sonny Jim!' he called as the doors closed.

Peter walked back over and gave the receptionist his card. 'Any problems or queries, give me a call; I'll pop by in the morning to make sure they aren't causing too much trouble.' Vasso gratefully took the card and thanked her lucky stars she'd be off duty before too long.

www.ingramcontent.com/pod-product-compliance
Lightning Source LLC
Jackson TN
JSHW031713220126
96620JS00002B/2
* 9 7 8 1 0 3 6 7 1 0 9 5 8 *